Making Life and Lemonade

Mamotladi Ivy Matloga

First Edition, 2019
ISBN: 978-1-77605-588-3
E-book: 978-1-77605-587-6

Cover design by Anita Stander
Layout and typesetting by Janet Von Kleist

Published by Kwarts Publishers 2019
www.kwartspublishers.co.za

To my mother,
Emily Mananyetso,
for your grace, love,
strength and wisdom.

About the author

Mamotladi Ivy Matloga

South African author and public servant, Mamotladi Ivy Matloga (née Mananyetso) was born in Mamphokgo, in the Limpopo Province. Mamotladi is the author of the contemporary novel, 'Madness in Duggart' (published in April 2017), which details the realities of mental illness in rural South Africa and is dedicated to her brother who copes with a mental illness. In 2017, Mamotladi contributed a short story titled: 'An African Christmas' to an anthology edited by Andrew Christie, titled Happy Holidays. She has also authored a Sepedi novel titled 'Mahlaku a Maswa', which was shortlisted for the 'I am a writer' competition by Human and Rossouw in 2007.

Goodbyes into the future

"Now tell me, Maki my girl, where does tomorrow sit in the space of your mind when you visualise it? What about next week and next year? When the future appears on your mental screen, do you see it above or in front of you? Do day and night do a round-about in your head only to come back exactly where you stand, as another day? Or do you perhaps need to stretch yourself to get to tomorrow? Tell me, is tomorrow not exactly where you are standing right now?"

Ntate, as we fondly referred to Dad, would occasionally throw this big question at any one of us. I always pictured a rosy, almost too bright future when he asked, but that I would not say.

"Ntate, through my mind's eye, I see days, weeks, months and years stacked on top of each other reaching for the skies. And then just as I think they might carry on for eternity in their upward movement, they unexpectedly make a turn at the end of the third decade, only to start the next one from the bottom again. That's how they seem like to me," I finally answered, taking care not to divulge to Ntate the exact details of a future I envisioned for myself whenever I saw the decades make a turn.

A mansion by the hills with a long driveway. A bunch of happy kids, freely running around. Slow romantic walks in our butterfly and bird haven of a garden. A big, luxuriously furnished office with magnificent views. These were not common fantasies for a rural girl like me. This is why I never shared my untamed desires with anyone – not my friends or my teachers, and certainly not my family. My dreams were mine to protect. Teacher Mpoifeng might not have known he'd taught me to guard my visions jealously when he laughed at my desk mate Lebo for daring to think she could be an accountant. But a lesson was learnt; by me.

Although Ntate passed away two decades ago, his test about how I view the future always gives me perspective on how I need to see the present in relation to the future. Today in relation to tomorrow. I wish I had asked him while he was alive what picture the metaphor was seeking to paint and exactly what message it intended to drive home. But I never did. Partly because this question was first presented to me when I was only eight years old and I must have gotten so used to it that, as I grew up, it became that question, that powerful yet meaningless question Ntate threw at us from time to time.

I also only ever attempted to answer it when I was about fifteen, after years of quiet contemplation. I still remember the particular day when I surprised him with an answer, and he smiled. I never bothered to get a much more helpful response because I could see the satisfaction in his smile – a particular contentment that I had dared to answer.

But there was another reason I never asked: Ntate only asked the question when he was a bit tipsy. That does not make me regret any less though, the fact that I did not ask and the undeniable truth that I would never get another chance at an answer. I just have to accept the fact that I will never know what lesson he wanted to pass on. What emotion he hoped to amass. At a deeper level, I truly do get it. There probably was no right or wrong answer to Ntate's question. No particular single meaning to it.

But exactly how the weighty words in this quiz blended and worked together in my mind to always achieve the kind of perspective I needed, I probably will never know.

But here they ring again as I prepare to assume a new managerial job in a couple of days, in a new organisation, leaving behind a field of expertise, an environment and work culture I had grown into, and a bunch of amazing colleagues whose company and team spirit I thoroughly delighted in.

Many that have changed jobs in pursuit of the proverbial greener pastures know that thorns are a natural part of the lush greens. They come in different shapes, sizes and spite.

Mpho, my manager for the past five years, is clearly happy for me, but I could sense a certain carefulness not to sound like she was discouraging this move. I'd read in between the lines, both the ones out of her mouth and those that curled up loudly on her forehead that very moment I told her about the new job I had accepted.

"I think I know exactly the person you will be reporting to," she had said. "I have worked with her in my previous life, and all I can say is, do not shrink for anyone; stay confident and strong, Maki. Please, allow no person to put punches in your spirit."

She did not have to say much to make me understand what her impressions of Lalang were. I did not know Lalang Masego; Mpho clearly did. I was afraid to dig, scared I might hear things I would rather not have heard. Besides, I was not going to withdraw from a position I've worked hard to obtain, anyway.

Putting together an application pack, being shortlisted and having had to prepare for an interview and two competency assessments was no mean feat. I filed the information from Mpho correctly so as to not affect my impressions of the woman who would be my boss or my ensuing work at the Commission for Public Affairs.

The coming month begins with a holiday on Monday, and I only get to start at my new job the day after. I will use the long weekend to prepare myself the best I know how, not deluding myself in any way about the challenge ahead of me and the fact that I could not at this stage have any answers to the myriad of questions that were bouncing up and down in my mind like the days do when I visualise the future. I ask myself what type of office environment and colleagues I was about to encounter. What exactly does Mpho know about Lalang that compelled her to say those encouraging words?

I cannot bring myself to thrust the key into the eager ignition. It will just remind me that this is it. I am about to drive away from my workplace, only for good this time around. The change that I had been craving for almost a year now had come not without a sting. I drop a tear as I pick up the charmingly designed farewell card on the passenger seat, then mull over the heartwarming send-offs from the colleagues I'd known for the past seven years – colleagues that have since become part of my life.

The messages are all special. But Hlomphanang's rings deeper:

> *"To my dear sister Maki. A sister among sisters! It goes without saying that I will miss you greatly, but I will tell you anyway. I will miss your beautiful soul, your grace, humbleness and warm smile. I will miss your gentle spirit, non-conforming yet inspiring nature, and your sense of humour. You will forever hold a special*

*place in my heart, and I will always be grateful to my
creator that I met someone like you."*

I shed a stream of tears as I recall how Hlomphanang tried
in vain to fight back a river of her own when she delivered
a personalised and well-considered farewell speech an hour
earlier, and how she had walked me to the parking lot
only to make a turn before I got to my car because it would
have been more painful to actually see me drive off. And
how she could not let go when she hugged me. I marvel
at the pureness of sisterly love as I wipe off the tears and
move on to the next message. It is from Mmagauta.

*"Maki, dearie, I will miss your leadership, your jokes,
your belly-crunching, tear-drenched laughter that
messed up your mascara, your playful spirit, and
motherly nature. I will also miss your sneezing. Jokes
aside, you are that manager I prayed for when I joined
this organisation – the best manager I could ever have
hoped for. I have been blessed."*

I manage to giggle a bit as I wipe a tear from my face. I had
completely given up on wearing mascara a few months
ago because it did not agree with my physiological reaction to laughter. The tears won.

My mind goes back to the sick office syndrome I am
hopefully leaving behind. I always sneezed while at work
but hardly ever sneezed outside of work. I hope that the
beautiful building that is going to be my new workplace
will be a much healthier space and not just a pretty face.

I look down once more at the card to read one from my
now former manager, Mpho. She writes matter-of-factly,
as always.

*"Maki, I wish I had something better to offer you.
I wish management had listened when I told them*

you were long ready for a promotion. I will miss your adeptness. I never had to worry when I received a report from you because I knew I was going to enjoy reviewing it; I will miss your analytical prowess, loyalty, hard work, your leadership of your team, and friendliness. I wish you everything of the best."

Another tear leads itself down to the very card. I know that asking for a manager as good as Mpho will probably be asking for a lot. But if my new manager could be half as supportive, then much of the battle would have been won.

I look around to absorb the air in the space for the last time — parking lot air that I often had to hold my breath to avoid inhaling. But today I have to take everything in to carry me along on Tuesday as I enter new premises, and the lives of people that are at this point, strangers. Did I make the correct move in this career game? Maybe I should have accepted the counter offer that Mpho was willing to negotiate with the powers that be. That way I would still be in my familiar territory and earning a higher salary than I was going to earn in my new job.

But I could not count on Mpho succeeding with the negotiations. Besides, the lure of a new venture had hit way too hard anyway, appearing too appealing to resist. It was more the new opportunity pulling than it was my existing one pushing me, and what a pull it was!

As I buckle up and finally manage to shove the key into the ignition, preparing to exit the building, I start to appreciate just how much I was leaving behind. For a brief moment, I question the wisdom of putting myself in such an uncomfortable situation. I look at some colleagues walking about outside the parking area, looking rooted and well-adjusted to this environment.

I force myself to choose to rather give myself a pat on the back for taking such a bold step to leave a comfort zone for a taste of the unknown. This is it. I now have to set up my mind not to blindly drive here on Tuesday morning. Come the next working day, when many go to their usual workplaces, I will be the lonely new face in the building — hopefully, one among a few new ones.

Would I be able to establish the same kind of connections in this new job that I had in that place I just walked out of that felt like a home away from home? What if those reporting to me had applied for this same position and were now bitter to not have bagged it? What if they are immature enough to take their frustrations and disgruntlement out on me? What if they set a trap for me or stabbed the air out of my tyres just as someone did to my friend, Tilly when she started in her new role as a manager amidst some bitter souls? What if they poisoned my lunch? Oh my gosh, I am going to have to keep my lunchbox in my car and make sure that, for the first week, I wear outfits with pockets so I can put my car keys inside too, at least until I know for sure I don't work with some evil sociopaths.

My husband's cousin was once poisoned at work, and he always makes sure to remind me just how sick some people can be. The cousin luckily survived. Someone else might not be so lucky, and that could well be me. At the risk of being called paranoid, I will keep my safety measures between my husband and I. Better safe than sorry.

My mother, Mantlo, raised us to not be afraid that we might be bewitched, but rather to be aware that poisoning is real and that people can actually perform that, but not some magic spell or witchcraft.

The workplace can easily become a war zone if people allow themselves to lose perspective. Society is racked by egotism, immaturity and greed. People become so power hungry and so obsessed with titles and money that they never stop to think of the actual reason any of us are employed.

When power and material benefits become driving forces behind what we do as workers, it is the poor that suffer. Service delivery is not always halted as a result of everyone dragging their feet or because they don't have a clue what they are doing.

Sometimes, often even, society suffers because it becomes so much about us workers, about what we stand to gain or lose. More lives get lost than those that get reported. Many workers suffer stress-induced illnesses. Many end up committing suicide. We have blood on our hands. All because someone else, and not us, got appointed to a higher position – the exact one we were eyeing and even banking on to lead us into the promised land, if not the cookie jar.

How much more self-seeking, shallow and short-sighted can it get? It makes me so sick when people are controlled by their zest for power and forget that their actions have enough power to send some poor soul to their grave prematurely. Just because you did not pull the trigger on someone does not make you any less of a killer when people collapse and die of heart attacks due to the stress that you have consistently piled on them. As human beings, we do not handle stressful situations in similar ways. We certainly do not process pain and disappointment the same way either. Still on criminality, how better are we than any cold-hearted criminal out there if someone dies because of a lack of service from us?

Still deep in thought, I catch myself pressing on the button of the remote control to open my garage door, and I wonder, with fear, how on earth I managed to find my way home with all the conversations in my head. It terrifies me because the last time I had been aware of my whereabouts was at the parking lot as I said goodbye to the bricks and the birds. I do not recall ever telling myself to now take that off-ramp, stop at that red traffic light or brake as the car in front of me braked. How did I get this far without having had to remind myself of the path I had to follow? Have I driven on this road so many times that I have now turned into a robot myself?

I truly respect, even revere the capacity of the human mind to store and retrieve information without so much as a rattle. At the same time, I get scared when I think of the dangers of unconsciously classifying oneself as an expert driver who does not need to go through the steps as they are already ingrained in one's mind.

Anyway, I am safely home. I cannot redo my ride. I park the car and reach for my phone which lay on silent mode inside the pocket of the driver's door. There is a text message — a reminder of my appointment at the spa on Sunday afternoon. I smile. I deserve this. I have not been to the spa in a while. Over the last six months, I had to be content with the soft foot massages my young son gave me as a reward for letting him play with my phone. "Remember my offer, Mom: foot massages every single day when you return home from work," Motheo had relentlessly offered until I could no longer resist. "My little steadfast negotiator," I say as he suddenly opens the car door and throws himself on me, arms outstretched in a welcoming embrace.

2

In with the new

I heard there are people who make major financial commitments based on jobs yet to be started, and on salaries yet to be earned. Some even do this on simple contract-less promises that could hardly be counted on.

I've heard of people taking their appointment letters to car dealerships to secure a new set of hot wheels to fit in with their ensuing new position. Unfortunately, this becomes the bottomless pit that traps people and keeps them entangled in the debt circle that promises them nothing but short-lived feelings of self-importance, which come short of hitting that sweet spot of fulfilment.

I ponder over this unfortunate phenomena as I envision myself getting pampered in preparation for my new job. I cannot help but thank my parents for having taught me not to live to impress, but instead to live within my means, without unnecessary self-deprivation.

For the next three to six months, if my lifestyle is to change based on my higher earnings, I would not allow it to be adjusted by the full difference in earnings. I would instead pretend to have half of the difference in earnings while pumping the other half into investments. Take half, leave half, as one financial management professor used to say.

I head for the beauty and health spa to get a relaxing aromatherapy massage that promises to take my mind off fretting and put me in a more positive mood for my big day and, hopefully, for some time to come.

I consider the enjoyment of the little things an amazing gift from above. For if one lacks the ability to glorify the source for the small indulgences provided, how is one ever to be afforded any bigger? I enjoy massages and would rather wear cheaper shoes and carry the same handbag every day just so I could have some money to enjoy that healing touch every once in a while. My friends at varsity never got used to the fact that a student could afford to treat herself to facials and massages, choosing those treats over a new pair of fashionable jeans.

I have left jobs and started new ones a couple of times before and getting a massage is my ritual to sort of take me out of the past and into the new. I have enough time to shop for an alternative outfit for my first day at the new job, so I take the route leading up to the mall.

I don't enjoy shopping for shopping's sake, but whenever there is an occasion to shop for, I tend to over prepare with at least two, but normally three outfits. This makes up for all the many non-shopping days. Though some of my friends think I'm boring for not having the same appetite for shopping as they do, I am content, for this is what I enjoy. Besides, the non-conformist in me is never satisfied with the norm and often deliberately opts to go left when everyone says going right is in fashion.

I love this soundless rebelliousness about me. In new jobs, colleagues would often be taken by surprise when they see me stand my ground for the first time. Their shock and usual "you're so humble; one could easily think they can walk all over you" got me to separate my trademark meekness from the no-nonsense girl. But it was my friend, Sofia, who decided I have an alter ego and together we decided to name her Ntsobe, which was the nickname I was given at primary school based on a character who was very small in appearance. Though I was never the smallest, my classmates wanted to remind me that I was actually the youngest in class.

Ntsobe and I have come a long way. She has saved me from potentially bad decisions in life, and from a lot of hurt. Even though I did not agree with Sofia at first that I should embrace the concept of an alter ego, I gradually warmed up to the idea and embraced it as soon as I made up my mind to differentiate between an alter ego and someone with multiple personality disorder. I love Ntsobe as much as I love Maki.

As a teenager, Ntsobe was always the one who would literally take my hand and leave whenever everyone said "you need to be like this or do this or that to move with the times, appear sophisticated or fit in".

If the trend was that one's shoes needed to match one's handbag to avoid some fashion crime, Ntsobe would analyse the logic and check whether or not she liked the idea, and if it tickled her fancy. If she didn't think it was attractive, appealing to her or sustainable, she would make sure I would never be caught with matching shoes and bags. It's about what makes sense to Ntsobe and not about what everyone is doing.

A formal but vibrant outfit jumps into sight as soon as I enter my favourite clothing outlet – the one that knows that women do come in different shapes and sizes, all of which deserve to be correctly catered for. I quickly take the outfit and head straight for the pay point.

Sometimes I shop like a man, and other times I don't. But I must have tried on outfits all of five times in my entire life – which frustrates Sofia as she's the type that would invite me to go and window shop and try on clothes.

My argument is that if any dress was going to embrace my curves, I could always tell by looking at it and I don't need to check for fit every time I buy an item. Besides, we all know how much bigger those fitting room mirrors make us. This is about the one thing that the fashion industry does that feels like lying, only in the customer's favour. If the industry revealed their true nature, everyone would look perfect in their outfits in order to push sales.

But then again, maybe they're avoiding the likely stream of returns that would occur when too many husbands become braver in answering the customary "does my butt look too big in this?"

I draw out my card to pay as the teller asks if I don't need an account. "No, thank you. I prefer this method of payment," I say, handing her my credit card.

She looks at me and smiles. "But you're using a credit card and not cash. You get charged a lot of interest this way. Better to open an account," she says confidently, sure to have made a scoring point.

"No, my dear sister, don't worry about that at all. I will never spend on this card more than I can afford to pay in full at the end of every single month," I respond, matching her confidence level.

She attempts to make up an answer but struggles either to formulate words or to get them out of her mouth. But she really did not need to, for her thoughts were boldly scripted all over her face. She didn't believe it was possible to pay off your credit card in full every month. Or maybe she didn't know that one can avoid being charged interest this way.

We say our cheerful goodbyes, and I leave, hoping to have positively affected one soul. I like that.

I park in front of the spa just in time for my treat. How I wish I wouldn't have to drive myself home after this treat. "If only I could be chauffeured after this," I fantasise as I step into the fantastic fusion of aromatherapy oil scents that hover gently in the air.

I instinctively inhale deeply. I could live with this. "I feel healed already," I say to myself, unaware I had actually blurted the words out loud until my favourite masseuse, Mmogeng, responds by saying: "We're so glad to hear that, Mrs Mako because we're in the business of healing. Please come through; you're right on time. Would you like anything to drink perhaps, before we begin?"

"Yes, water please." I say with a smile, trying hard to contain the itch to tell her for the hundredth time just how beautiful her name is. The last time I did I got a sense that she must be hearing that all the time – maybe from me all the time. Her name means 'look at her' but in a much more pageantry way that says 'admire her; look at her, in adoration'.

"No ice, Sesi," Mmogeng informs the general assistant on my behalf as she asks her to bring me a glass of water. I commend her for knowing me so well as to be able to speak for me when I forget to do so myself.

"Who could forget just how much you love your warmth, Mrs Mako. And how much you cannot stand coldness in all its forms!"

Sesi returns with a glass of water. But it has ice in it. I'm not sure whether she might not have registered it as the request for no ice did not come from me, or maybe her mind was just somewhere else today.

"Sesi, please also bring me a glass, but mine shouldn't have ice, please," Mmogeng says.

Not catching on, I add "please bring me another glass without ice, too".

As Sesi leaves, Mmogeng points out to me that her tender request was actually on my behalf. I laugh at myself. I'm not used to this level of slowness, you know. How could I not have caught on? Being a Virgo, I probably would be criticising myself about this for months if not years to come.

If people realised just how hard I can be on myself, that I am my own harshest critic, they would probably see no need to criticise me at all. The nit-picker in me is getting me to be anxious now. This is the worst time to be slow; I need all my confidence for the new job. I come back and catch myself being overly critical about something that most people would not even have revisited past the initial laughter. I hate this perfectionist mentality and, as I hate to remind myself, the veiled ego that fuels it, as some experts believe.

The self-lashing dissolves as soon as Mmogeng puts her magical, schooled hands on my feet. My thighs await eagerly for their turn. I take a deep breath to bring myself into the present. "Do people sometimes cry tears of joy when you massage them?" I ask through my soft moans as her skilful hands touch a hundred right spots all at once. She had told me before she enjoyed massaging meaty customers like me, and as she presses, I don't have to wonder in guilt whether those extra layers are presenting any added burden to her overworked hands.

"Crying does happen at times, especially when one has a lot of pain bottled up inside, and as the tension melts away, so do they." I ponder a bit, digging deeper to find out if the slight need to let go of what I thought would be tears of joy, may, in fact, indicate any deep-rooted pain. I decide the answer to be no, and slip into a soft relaxing sleep, hoping to wake up the next morning on my bed.

I doubt if my subconscious would ever allow me to deceive myself by pretending that some strong men would lift me up from the massage bed to the car, drive me home and carry me to my bed on a palanquin like I was Cleopatra the Queen. I would probably need to be hypnotised to reach that level of fantasy. In my real world, I still have to wake up and face the reality that I don't have a driver and will have to drive, as carefully as I can, the pothole-infested ten-kilometre journey between the spa and my home.

I tip Mmogeng, and she is as thankful as she is surprised. I don't know when she will begin to move away from her usual 'tipping is something that is usually practiced by wealthy clients, and they are mostly paler in complexion' comment. I smile and tell her as I exit, that I love acting wealthy sometimes as it gives me good vibrations.

Though I can hardly wait to get home, I decide that nothing and no one on the road was going to get on my nerves in any way, shape or form. That, of course, includes the hungry potholes that are big enough to swim in, and the annoyingly slow driver in the fast lane, who for all I know, could be suffering from a bad case of piles — *poor thing*. I exclaim as I move to the left lane to pass the driver, manoeuvring to avoid an eager pothole at the same time. Beats me why they even bother to warn us of these holes that are so huge they can be seen from space!

A few years ago, while recovering from an operation, I'd vowed to never again be impatient on the road with 'slow drivers'. My slow walking movements at the time translated into super slow driving as every change of gear, and every blind spot check felt like I was attempting to actually run to my destination at high speed.

I inhale a lung-full of the sweet-smelling oils on my skin, hold and breathe out. I couldn't care less if every single driver on the road today was having some sort of pain on their lowermost areas, I was still going to drive without hitches and arrive home unmoved.

I get home and sleep like a sweet baby until around half past nine on Monday morning. Thank goodness for these occasional public holidays. My husband could just as well not have slept in the bed; I did not hear him come to bed, and certainly did not hear him get out of bed.

I reach for my phone and go through a sea of text messages. One from an acquaintance reads: "welcome to the month of July".

I smile and respond with a thank you. But the truth is, I wonder whether some people arrive in new months before the rest of us, so they can stand at the entrance and dutifully give us late-comers warm welcomes. Did my waking up late make me the last one to get into July? Is anyone fit to welcome me to a month, really? I wonder. I start to think about which of the twelve months I could welcome people into. Maybe my birth month, or the first month in winter because people would appreciate some warmth to carry them through the cold months ahead. But who wants to be welcomed into cold weather, more layers of clothing, and shorter days?

I decide I will just accept the welcomes. After all, they only happen twelve times a year. Which reminds me that my salary, too, follows the same pattern.

Another message from a friend is more than a welcome. It says best wishes for July. Now this one I will happily feast on for days to come.

3

Those first impressions

Besides being grateful for starting my new job on a Tuesday and having a four-day work week, I'm also thankful to be starting during the school holidays while the kids are away visiting their grandparents. This is a perfect time to begin a new job, in every way I can think of.

The worrywart that I usually am, I'm happy that at least I don't have to worry myself sick and spend a sleepless night wondering if the alarm will go off as ordered and what would happen if my Plan B wake-up call that is my husband, oversleeps. I know it never happens because he seems to have an internal alarm clock, which I suspect could have something to do with the benevolent bird that – on the rare occasions when I happened to have woken up earlier – I could hear knocking on our bedroom window, seemingly at the same time, every time.

Makhananisa insists he is just a natural early bird himself and needs no actual birdie to act as his alarm. But as far as I'm concerned, if he was ever to oversleep, it was going to be on a day like this when I so need him to wake up at his usual time, should the alarm not kick in as expected, or the birdie forgets to knock. Some call it Murphy's Law; I just call it life. My husband would say it simply is what worrying knows to attract.

I manage to get some sleep despite having gone to bed making senseless and step-less calculations about what my first day at the new office would be, feel, sound, smell and taste like.

I somehow wake up knowing which of my three equally beautiful and curve-hugging outfits I am supposed to wear. But as I flaunt it in front of my husband, instead of the usual 'yeah baby' approval, he points out that despite looking great, the outfit is too bold for a first day on the job.

I shrug my shoulders in an apparent defeated move and ask him if his opinion has anything to do with jealousy. But I'm already undressing even before he answers. Maybe because I somehow can see where he is coming from. "I can always wear it once the first impressions have been formed," I say matter-of-factly.

I decide what to wear, and it's not going to be any of the two other new outfits. I don't fight the decision. My habit of wearing new clothes to a new job was after all not as static as I had thought. And it was not so painful to divert from. "Sofia would literally come all the way to force me into one of the three new outfits," I say as I make swift turns in front of the mirror. "Do me a favour, Doll; show them you've got great fashion sense and do it from the onset. We do not want them to start whispering that you only started dressing well after your first pay," my friend instructed me on a call just the previous morning.

"I would rather go there in less than showy attire and uncover who is true and who is superficial," Makhananisa says.

"You make a good point there, my darling," I respond, nodding my head.

"My love, I know you understand that kind of thing. Are you not the one who always says if you were a well-to-do guy you would present a less than wealthy facade on a date and assess how materialistic your date is?" he adds.

"Yes, I would even rent a run-down vehicle to pick up my date. I'd be the perfect gentleman during the date, of course. But I'll be on the lookout for any signs of materialism. And if the girl concludes that I'm not worthy of another date, I would then call my driver and pretend the car was broken and they must come pick us up in 'that one'. We would drop her off at her place, and I would say 'thank you for the lovely evening; I wish you all the best. You'd be surprised, some of these money-oriented girls would dare to call after having clearly stated there was no way there would ever be a second date."

"That doesn't sound right, though," my husband says laughing.

"You look amazing," Makhananisa assures me.

I'm glad there aren't any kids to get ready for school today. Much as I enjoy bathing my young ones every day until they are able to bathe themselves, it can be daunting at times. It affects the clothes I choose to wear, and how I apply my make-up, if at all. Today I can look like a peacock if I choose to, except I know it's not the appropriate look for my field of work, especially for creating that everlasting first impression. It's very easy to end up with a nickname like 'peacock,' you know.

As I prepare my lunchbox, Makhananisa stops me. "My darling, leave that, let's go. I'll take you out for lunch today." Before I could remind him that I would likely not have the luxury of a lunch date on my first day at the job, he comes to his senses and says, "Look, I'll buy lunch and deliver it to you." And so he did, for a good week. Not only dropping off the meals but keeping me company during my lunchtimes. I didn't care much about how the boxed meals might ruin my recently-acquired two-kilos less look. I was only thankful for my thoughtful husband's consideration. Heavens knew I would need his familiar voice to break my day. The lunchtime connection would come in handy given the loneliness at the new job and the disconnectedness I was to experience.

It is a blessing that he works only a few streets away from my new workplace, and we can use one car until the schools reopen. At least I don't have to worry about finding a spot to park my car before permanent parking could be arranged for me. I can also just sit back and be driven to and from work, for a change.

I get directed to the security unit as soon as I introduce myself to the receptionist as a new employee. But not before she asks where I worked before. I answer, and she could hardly contain her alarm.

"I am surprised that anyone would want to leave that organisation to come work here. Many of us want to leave this place, but you just left such a prestigious company to come and work here!" she says, shaking her head like a concerned parent who could say no more as she felt that she had made her point in reprimanding a wayward teenager.

I make light of her concerns and respond by jokingly saying that every workplace, every esteemed office block, has its own ghosts and unfortunately one only gets to know this once one is already in. As much as I loved my previous job and organisation, there were ghosts there too. They exist in every company.

"The trouble in this place is just caused by one person who sits up there. If that one can go, this place will function like a well-oiled machine. One woman only needs to retire," she adds. I do not probe for names.

I would need to have my employee access card sorted out, among other things, before someone takes me up to my new workstation on the third floor.

I immediately sense that my new manager might not be very popular in the organisation, or maybe just not with the security staff. I conclude after I get rewarded with simultaneous crippling laughs from the three security guards behind the desks as I respond to a seemingly innocent question by one of the three: "who are you going to be working with?"

"Who is she going to work with?" Asks the fourth guard who was sitting at a distance and had missed my answer.

"With ... with Lalang," the one helping me responds, breaking out in laughter in between his words as he anticipates the same reaction from his colleague, and then joining him as he contributes his own share of belly-crunching, whistling laugh. He has the kind of piercing laugh that makes you feel as though he is actually laughing at you. I do my best not to internalise it. I know they all are laughing at whatever they knew to laugh at about anyone, not necessarily myself, possibly having to work with Lalang.

The situation reminds me of what an old colleague at my sister's job said to her when she was a newcomer. "I see you are still walking in high heels, my dear. Trust me; you will soon be wearing flat shoes like the rest of us. All we're going to afford you is this first week; then you'll be flattened, dear sister. The thorns here burn as they prick."

Noticing my dismay, the guard turns to me and says "worry not, my dear sister, you will soon find out. Just do not worry your pretty face at all about the things hidden within the invisible cracks of these seemingly perfect walls. We just happen to have been working here for way too long, and we know where those cracks are, when and how they got to be formed; we even know how to make them appear and disappear in our minds. And that right there is the problem with old furniture, my sister. Forgive us for laughing. Don't let us derail you. You are most welcome in this place," he says, his cheeks still somewhat ballooned as he tried in vain not to alarm me any further.

Never being one to judge people based on others' perceptions of them, I quickly dismiss the officials' loud insinuations about my new manager as I turn to greet the lady that had just walked in, apparently to usher me into the building. I smile and say goodbye to the security officers, and following the lady in and out of the elevator, I finally make my entrance, bright-eyed and bushy-tailed, into my new office space.

In the elevator, I had started to recognise the usher as the same lady that invigilated over the selection test. I search my heart and find no fond memories of her at all. But I will give her a chance.

As I think about the awkward small talk I felt to make in the lift and how I had hoped she would have initiated it herself, my mind elects to revisit my memories of my accomplice, if only to fill the huge space in between the short awkward conversations we have so far managed in what had felt like a ride through thirty floors, with stops at each single one.

"Ten minutes left," the lady had pompously alerted us on the day as all three candidates paused and looked at her, seemingly examining as I also was, her body language and the self-important energy she exuded as she talked and even as she walked across the room with her shoulders high up. I'd even caught one of the candidates as she rolled her eyes and made a 'goodness gracious me' face after staring at our invigilator.

My new colleague's whole aura had been off-putting that day. I have just learnt that her name is Maphefo and she is one of the highly experienced junior managers, having been in her position for nearly a decade.

Later I would learn that Maphefo is also a bit bitter about being a junior manager and tends to attempt to outshine and outsmart any new senior managers. I also quickly witness that she is a know it all who criticises almost everything that anyone else does or says.

But thou shalt not judge. I choose to erase every little negative realisation and piece of information. I will still give Maphefo a chance. After all, she greeted me with a warm smile and a hug, and that went a long way to making me feel welcome despite our long pauses in the lift. On top of that, she will be reporting to me. Maphefo proceeds to introduce me to the rest of the team members.

"Does she not remind you of Amy?" Maphefo asks my new manager as she points me in the direction of my workstation. I glance at the manager probably more than I should as I try to find any hint of why the mention of her name could have evoked considerable laughter from the security staff.

I remember her from both my verbal and written interviews.

"No!" the manager responds with rather an excessive disagreement at the comparison. Curious to know who this Amy that I am being likened to and strongly not being likened to was, I ask, "Who is Amy?" The manager, who has now officially introduced herself to me as Ms Lalang Masego, responds by dismissingly saying "it is some ... woman who used to be in the same office you're going to be using," she responds pointing to the adjacent office and following her answer with a silly, haughty laugh, which Maphefo knowingly joins without hesitation.

How bizarre, I think to myself, that the same person whose name made other people laugh downstairs was now also laughing at the mention of somebody else's name. Somebody that used to report to her. Is this some unwritten part of the organisational culture to burst out laughing at the mention of people's names? Well, it all remains to be seen.

But what is now clear to me is that this Amy woman's departure, maybe even her stay in this office, was likely not a pleasant one. What was also clear was that there was some form of collective silliness at play around here, at least between the two ladies. It mattered not what this Amy lady might have been like or how their working relationship was, the kind of facial expression that Lalang displayed, and the sarcastic laugh she uttered following her brusque answer to my question about Amy, spoke of vast insensitivity and immaturity.

Could this be the reason the security guards also laughed when I told them I was going to work with Lalang? Only time will tell. I have to remain positive and unaffected. I was not going to take anything at face value, nor was I going to allow myself to be influenced by others' opinions of anyone's character, ability, or any perceived lack thereof. I was to be open-minded, open-hearted and obtain my own, unaffected perspective of situations.

We learn through experience, and to be a good leader one must have been led at some point in one's career, whether well or poorly. In one of my previous jobs, a new manager joined the organisation and immediately requested one-on-one meetings with staff according to a schedule she had drawn up and communicated to all of us.

The schedule had rightfully included all staff members. After meeting with the first two officials, however, the manager strangely abandoned the one-on-one sessions and immediately developed an undesirable attitude towards the rest of the officials, with the exception of the two she had met with. No one ever knew what she may have been told by the two colleagues, but since those two always had a reputation for flattery, sucking up and backbiting, the rest of us just sort of knew we had been artfully smeared.

From this experience, I decided that when the time comes for me to be entrusted with a management responsibility one day, I was not going to form opinions about others based on what someone else might have whispered in my ear. I vowed to be careful of those that would come to me with horrible paintings of others. The best option was still to talk to people and to gradually learn from them about them, understanding their weak and strong points, and helping them bring their best to the party, instead of judging them based on opinions of usually ambitious, self-seeking individuals.

Two-way communication will always beat the one-way conversations we have with ourselves about others. And it will hands down beat the gossip we choose to entertain, which hardly ever serves well the interests of those we are supposed to be serving.

Workplaces can be very unwelcoming, even poisonous, places for introverted individuals like me who just want to do their job, be of service, without having to position themselves as the boss's favourite by constantly feeding what would quite often be bottomless egos. I have learnt that being introverted works well where the boss does not thrive on cronyism and gossip mills. And so far it does not appear to me that I was in luck, as Lalang quickly leads me into her office to dish out my marching orders, which to my surprise, had very little to do with work.

"You see Maki, if a person is good to me, I am good to them in return. If you treat me well, I will take very good care of you," she says, slightly beating her chest with her hand as if to make some kind of oath.

The utterance takes me aback because I would have thought such things are human nature and mainly should go without saying. Having to go to the extent of pronouncing it sounds to me more like the idiom, "you scratch my back, and I'll scratch yours," and it only serves to make me more uncomfortable, to say the least. Even in my discomfort, I take refuge in the fact that the statement did not come from someone of the opposite sex because I probably would have classified it as possible harassment.

I drag my heavy head out of Lalang's office and head for my new one. The burnt orange walls pretend to suck me in as I ruminate over the packed hour since I entered through the doors of the organisation. The spooks here seem raw and unparalleled. I need to afford myself some privacy and cleanse the air around this office with my prayers. Whatever curses and demons exist in here would never get a taste of me. There is so much to pray about. If my days are going to be filled with so much drama, snobbery, and vagueness, I sure will be needing my God even more than I thought. If I did not know it before, now I do. I realise that in my anxiety about starting a new job, I had not set out time to pray this morning.

My thoughts and questions to myself about the environment, Lalang's vague comments, the security officials, the Receptionist, Amy, the crazed double laughs, and Maphefo's long years of service in the same position are interrupted by a hardly perceivable knock on the door.

"I really needed some alone time," I moan softly as I feel a bit anxious that I may not get a chance to rid the office space of the eerie evil forces that were, without a shadow of a doubt, present. It can be daunting being an excited new employee. You come in as that proverbial new broom that is ready to sweep ever so cleaner, happy to meet new people, oblivious to the many that are thinking to themselves behind the smiles as they shake your hand, "welcome, you poor thing, to the real wild-wild-west. If only you knew how hard we all are working at leaving this organisation, you wouldn't have allowed yourself to be lured here. We hope you have multiple belts fastened because you are in for the ride of your life; no one likes working here, especially with this manager".

I pull the slightly open door towards me. It is Faith, one of the employees I've just been introduced to. Though I could not grasp everyone's faces and names, Faith's warm, receptive smile made her easy to remember, and I had asked for her name again and fixed it to memory. She's one of the middle managers and she, like Maphefo, will report to me.

After the earlier hurried introduction, she saw it proper to steer her wheelchair to my office to give me an unhurried welcome, assure me of her undivided support and wish me well in my new position. I consider myself a fairly good judge of character and Faith seems like a genuinely nice person. I appreciate her visit despite having my prayer interrupted before it even started.

My guess is that Faith must have applied for this post because her position as the middle manager was just a rank below mine. But if I was feeling a little apprehensive about someone having been denied an opportunity for a promotion and then taking it out on me, Faith made me feel a tad safer. She looks happy and content even in her apparent infirmity. I've always had a soft spot for people with disabilities. Ever since I was placed in a hospital ward as an able-bodied child alongside five children, all with various disabilities, when I was just four years old, I had always yearned to work with less abled people. And somehow I always gravitate towards them and they, too, seem drawn to me. Maybe it also has to do with my being a fan for the underdog in every situation. I choose not to get overly excited though. It was still early days.

Yet, I cannot help but wonder what Lalang was on about when she criticised Faith earlier on when I was in her office. I was already forming an opinion about Lalang, and it was not the most positive of opinions. The security guards' reaction, her soulless answer to my question about who Amy was, the arrogant laugh that followed her answer about Amy, the insinuation that if I'm nice to her she'll be nice to me, her untimely critique concerning Faith, saying that she didn't know what to do with 'that person', and of course my former manager, Mpho's words upon learning I'll be working with Lalang. It was too much to digest, and it was not even lunchtime yet. It was only my first day on the job, and already the evidence that

I was probably not in the most peaceful or considerate environment was just overwhelming.

Why would anyone, any manager, talk so badly about an employee and refer to them as a burden? I don't care what Faith was able or unable to do, Lalang's behaviour was extremely uncivilised and childish. My phone rings and I answer, prompting Faith to say her goodbyes. It's my welcome break – my dear hubby calling from outside the building to bring my lunch. My sanity craved this break. 'Brace yourself, Mr Mako! Do I have one big pile of short stories to share with you,' I mutter into the credenza as I shut and lock my handbag inside.

Good thing we're breaking the day's events into two. I don't know if I would have been able to carry everything through to the end of the day. My voice would not have been able to convey the full day's occurrences in one evening. Later on, we will only deal with the second half.

Into the Deep End

Like most managers starting a new job, I've been expected to hit the ground running, and to continue to chew my gum as I ran. I was, however, not very pleased with the manner in which reporting lines were disrespected and how communication happened. I wouldn't consider myself to be title or even rank-conscious, but I couldn't accept the fact that Maphefo made all the decisions about what meeting I was supposed to attend, where and when, without so much as a discussion with me. She wasn't my personal assistant – I didn't have one. It was such a bitter pill to swallow and even attempting to swallow it for the time being was a painful exercise. The modus operandi was foreign to me.

I had accepted that Maphefo reported directly to me and not to Faith as the component structure and standard protocol dictated. As to the reason for the unusual reporting arrangements, Lalang mumbled something about infighting going on within the unit, especially between Maphefo and Faith, who loathed each other like light and darkness. But the reporting arrangement was already proving to be troublesome because it was clear that Maphefo called the shots within the unit.

This was the point where all the animosity between Lalang and myself began. I had hoped to gain perspective when I approached Lalang to clarify the span of control and how communication needs to happen compared to how it actually happens between all of us.

I had already noticed that when Lalang came back from meetings with her superiors, or with anyone for that matter, the first, and usually the only person she would brief and give feedback to, would be Maphefo. Never myself or Faith, who were both senior to Maphefo. I also realised that a familiar communal laughter was always at the centre of their feedback sessions. "You should have seen her, Maphefo. You know, today she's wearing some lousy skirt that could well have belonged to her grandmother in nineteen what-the-heck. That Kaitlyn desperately needs a stylist," Lalang would say. When they finished assessing Kaitlyn's fashion sense and a lack of it, they would start criticising her intelligence. "You don't say; a whole senior manager doesn't know that!" Maphefo would loudly belt out following whatever gossip Lalang would have shared with her about Kaitlyn or any other person that Lalang would have been in a meeting with. The gossip-fuelled laughter was the order of the day, I soon would realise, and try to accept.

On rare occasions I would be afforded a feedback session, but only after Maphefo has received the lowdown. But many times I would be forgotten. Not even my visit to her office after she was done with Maphefo qualified me as deserving of feedback from Lalang's meetings, some of which I would later learn I should have rightfully been invited to.

What bothered me was that often after the non-briefings, Lalang would write me an email starting with the words "as indicated" or "as discussed with you," before she broke the news and outlined expectations to me, for the very first time. When it first happened, I dismissed it as an honest mistake and didn't mention in my response to her that the contents weren't discussed with me before. However, as the trend continued, and I was witnessing more and more mismanagement, I started pointing out the seemingly calculated errors. She did not apologise or defend herself when I did; she just carried on with her apparent confusion between who Maki was and who Maphefo was, and who actually was her direct subordinate. And having observed that I, as the second in charge, was practically the one way down the ladder in terms of the true span of control, I started believing that she somehow mistook Maphefo for me because she continued to brief her and not me, and carried on with her 'as discussed' emails.

In one of our earlier meetings, Lalang even tried to attach all blame to me: "I need to be able to differentiate between you and the junior officials". She conveniently forgot that she was the one making the distinction difficult. There was still Faith who ranked higher than Maphefo, and she too was never kept in the loop. She too was being ignored. Invisible. Yet Lalang expected us to be up to date with any new developments.

As Faith and I started opening up to each other, she told me that Lalang hands out every available opportunity for training to Maphefo and gives her the exposure, and then she would elevate her in meetings saying she is very good at her work and better than most officials at senior level.

As a result, Maphefo would walk with her shoulders higher and higher up in the air, her head growing bigger. And together, mentor and mentee would continue to claim for themselves the conjoined position of the organisation's intellectuals. I could not help but wonder why on earth Lalang never seized the opportunity to promote her protégé when she recently had not one, but two opportunities she could have used.

But I couldn't say this to Faith; all I could do as a manager was to listen to her problems and promise to take them up with Lalang. But before I could get a chance to raise Faith's concerns, I stepped on the snake's tail by highlighting the error in Lalang's communication strategy, much to her anger.

"I do not have to tell you anything. May I remind you, I do not report to you, Ma'am," Lalang arrogantly pointed out to me.

"I was merely asking whether there was anything I could do to make it easier for you to update me after your meetings, or better still, to invite me to some of the meetings," I reply, suppressing the urge to just remind her of the fact that she often makes the mistake of saying we have discussed issues when we have not discussed anything. The frequent error to me indicated that she was aware that it was proper to discuss.

"I choose which meetings to invite you to and which ones to go to on my own; I cannot be dictated to by you, Maki. You don't even come to my office; how do you expect me to communicate with you? You know, where there is no communication, there is no trust. Absolutely no trust."

"I understand that we need to find a way to communicate better. But we need not lose sight of the fact that communication is a two-way process. What I can deduce is that our communication styles might be at odds, which is why we don't communicate as well as we should be. And because there is nothing wrong with being different, the best we can do is to find some common ground so that we can be able to work better together."

"You know, Maki. Me, I will never *skinder* about you, ever! But if you don't like me, I really have no problem at all. I do not wake up in the morning intending to establish a friendship with you," Lalang retorts, teary-eyed with a shaky voice, and wearing a nasty look.

I am startled. I have only been in the organisation for two months, and already things are snowballing this far south! I compose myself and manage to respond: "It's not that I don't like you, Ma'am," I say, making sure to 'ma'am' her back and then watch her as the 'ma'am' sinks in. Certain that it hit almost the same spot as hers did mine, I continue: "I have no room for hatred in me, Ms Masego. I don't know what could possibly have made you think I dislike you, because I don't. As for forming a friendship, I think when that happens in a working environment, it can be a special, even productive thing. But friendships happen organically and I never for a moment expected any friendship from you. This, of course, is different from being friendly, kind, and even civil.

"I do come to your office, but you still withhold information from me. Moreover, you have this unwelcoming look about you that always makes me think twice about voluntarily coming to your office. But my biggest concern is the withholding of important information. Sharing information should not depend on visits, friendliness or a lack thereof."

"Which look are you talking about? It is my nature; it's how I am."

"Okay, I am glad you explained that. Now that I know, I will no longer take it to heart and will come freely into your office. But I would like to be invited to some of the meetings you attend. You know, when I meet other colleagues, and I tell them I work in this unit, they ask why I was not at this meeting or that one. It has happened twice already. It unsettles me and renders me an outsider in a way. I don't think it makes the unit look good either. People don't know me yet, but through you, I can gain a foothold in the other organisational functions. Anyone entering an organisation starts at a certain level of incompetence, and it may take some mentoring to get them to develop."

I left Lalang's office with mixed emotions. I'm glad that we ironed out certain things, but I'm not sure how I feel about some of her utterances. Is it really necessary to tell your colleague that you do not come to work to be friends with them? Friendships at work happen when people click, and though she and I do not, I don't see any necessity in pointing it out. I'm also not certain that her disgusted look won't keep me out of her office anymore. But I'm glad that I spoke to her about including me in her meetings. The reason we are here, after all, has nothing to do with ourselves.

But Lalang did not suddenly start briefing me, nor did she start extending meeting invitations to me. The rest of us all had to resort to eavesdropping as Lalang and Maphefo gossiped and degraded people following Lalang's meetings with just about anyone inside or outside the organisation. Maphefo would humour Lalang with her usual: "ah, really? A senior official said that? One cannot help but wonder how some people get these senior management positions".

This would always be followed by the most scornful of laughs. Of course in the company of the same officials they laughed at, Lalang and Maphefo would smile from cheek to cheek and fake as though their lives depended on it.

But where Lalang started to look at me from the corners of her shadowy eyes was when I talked to her about the poor communication that involved Maphefo deciding meetings on my behalf, without any input or consultation from my side whatsoever. I highlighted the incidents that signalled to me that there was an issue — first, the invitation to a component meeting, one that I headed, coming from Maphefo, a couple of weeks into the job. I'd felt uncomfortable but obliged to attend. After all, an important work document relating to a project that was underway was to be discussed at the meeting.

Though I was unhappy with the fact that Maphefo did not bother talking to me first about either the document or my availability for the meeting, I decided to honour it. After all, I was still learning the culture of the organisation, and for all I knew, this could simply be part of that culture and nothing to do with anything else.

I chaired the meeting, as I did the previous one that Maphefo convened on my behalf a few days after my assumption of duty. I quickly learnt that any meetings that involved brainstorming were thorny territory in Lalang's unit. Maphefo and Faith went for each other's throats right from the beginning, and about the most mundane of issues. I could see that the meeting was not going to be fruitful, so I closed the session about half an hour later when my efforts to get the two to respect each other's views, continuously fell on unfertile ground. I had not known the two colleagues for long and had to be careful to draw conclusions based on my observations thus far.

I needed some time to digest everything that just happened, to hopefully identify the root causes of the issues and to address them, once and for all. So I adjourned the meeting, having called on everyone to go and reflect on what had happened, and hopefully meet again the next day when we were calmer and more clear-headed. I had no doubt in my mind that I was capable of remedying whatever ills haunted the team. Love, both pure and tough, empathy, respect, impartiality and sensitivity were to be ingredients in my healing recipe.

It was after this particular meeting that I'd decided to visit Lalang's office to gather some intelligence about what had happened. Like someone who had lost any hope of things ever changing for the better, she'd told me that the infightings were the very reason why Maphefo doesn't report to Faith. "They fight even in front of external stakeholders during workshops. I don't see them ever getting along," she said softly, sounding every bit like a woman defeated.

* * *

Instead of the follow-on team meeting, I decide to send two separate meeting requests to the two colleagues for the following day. I am determined to address the animosity.

First I meet with Maphefo. After we exchange some pleasantries, I ask her if she had always reported to Lalang. She tells me that she used to report to Amy, but when Amy left, she reported to Lalang.

"Why didn't you report to Faith when Amy left?" I ask because Lalang is three ranks above Maphefo. Maphefo's body language warned me to tread carefully.

"I don't see myself growing under Faith's direction. You should hear the kind of mistakes she makes and the misinformation she gives to people when she presents.

"I have nothing personal against Faith. But I would rather report to Lalang again than have to report to Faith – that's if you don't like the idea of me reporting to you. In this place, we report to whomever we want to report to. There is no flat reporting structure like you find in many organisations."

I could sense that a cemented opinion had been formed and it would take a concerted effort to undo. Especially because even the head herself seems to support it. Fish truly does rot from the head. I ask Maphefo if she appreciates that Faith is relatively new to the unit and that there would be certain things that Maphefo would know, which someone like Faith, or myself for that matter, would need time and exposure to grasp.

I ask her if she agrees that it is important to listen to another person's viewpoint and to present one's own in a manner that does not degrade the other person or ridicule their view.

"People just do not read. That's the main problem. People are so lazy," she says with bulging eyes, shrugged shoulders and stretched out hands with her fingers pointing upwards to give support to her shoulders.

My attempt at playing psychologist was not yielding much of a positive outcome. So I ask Maphefo if she would be open to us getting some form of professional assistance that would mend the broken pieces of her relationship with Faith.

"I don't need that; I am okay where I'm at as far as our relationship is concerned. I am at peace with everything," she says. I watch her as she acts out her words; her over-confidence heavily leaning to the side of condescension.

Her stance as far as getting professional assistance does not surprise me much. When I spoke to Lalang about getting an internal mediator, she too had brushed that off by saying: "we have tried everything and nothing is ever going to work for those two."

I conclude my meeting with Maphefo; take a tea break and ask Faith to come in. Faith is as deeply hurt as I had observed previously. I ask Faith what in her mind she would like to see done to mend the injured relationship.

"As long as the one on top is still full of favouritism and silliness, I do not see things getting to normal. Mind you, Maphefo hated me from the moment I stepped in, and for two years I greeted her warmly every morning hoping she would one day accept that I was here, but she never greeted me herself when she was in a position to be the one doing the greeting. So I decided to stop trying. I think she wanted this post and still does.

Where Maphefo exhibited pomposity, Faith did pain. Lots of it. "You know, I would be presenting in a workshop, and she would put her head in her hands – those gestures affected me quite a lot. At one point she disagreed with me in front of the audience as though we were not part of the same team. What I can tell you, Maki, is that there's no team here, there's only meat," Faith says. She too sounding defeated, but not in the same way Lalang did the previous day.

Then, like a scratched record, she starts repeating the issues she had already told me. About how all opportunities are given to Maphefo – be it high-level meetings that would give her visibility and exposure, or training courses and conferences that would keep her abreast of industry developments.

Then she starts to cry as she relates how in the past she had been excluded even from internal unit meetings and how during one rare attendance as she voiced out her concerns about not getting exposure, Lalang responded by saying 'we only send people that have job experience and knowledge to these conferences.' "Tell me, how will I ever gain the same level of know-how and experience if I'm always excluded?"

It is a tricky situation. I am reminded of a graduate who once wrote in his Curriculum Vitae, under the heading 'job experience': 'how do you expect me to gain experience if you're not willing to give me that experience in the first place?' The unnerving thing is that I see for myself some of the things that Faith is crying about, and I have, in my relatively short time here, already asked the same questions that she was asking.

I have observed how Maphefo and Lalang attended meetings, workshops, and conferences without ever thinking to extend invitations to the rest of the personnel.

I find myself caught up between a very rough rock and an extremely hard place. Being at the receiving end of these happenings myself, I am seriously stuck!

She suddenly stops crying. "You have been a blessing to me, Maki, because I can see you have humility, and you are fair. It has not been easy at all for me. Two years ago I wanted to quit this job to go start my own business without a proper plan in place because waking up in the morning to come to work had become one tall order that I could feel would eventually kill me. Angela at Human Resources discouraged me from doing so. She sat me down and advised me not to resign out of frustration. She really helped me because I don't know how I would have managed, with kids still at school and both going to varsity in a couple of years. I cannot forget that lady's words."

She pauses to push back some tears that were beginning to build up inside her big, brown eyes before carrying on. "She said to me: 'Faith, we work in this office and we have seen many resign without any concrete plans to support their livelihoods, all because of difficult and seemingly unmanageable work situations. And many of them have come to regret their hasty moves. This place is nobody's private business, and no one is Pty. Limited here. You may leave today because of them, only to learn next month that they have accepted a job at another organisation and left.

You really need to go buy yourself a thicker skin, my sister. No one pays your salary here. We all stand in the same queue to receive our salaries from the same coffers. If for whatever reason you do not get paid come month-end, your manager too would be facing the same predicament. Do not worry when they treat you badly. By you leaving your position, they would have won in more ways than one.

Firstly, they would have gotten rid of you, and secondly, the position would now be there for the taking. No matter how hard it is, continue to do your work as best as you can, not for those that torture you but for the masses that pay your salary and benefit from your services. Get some counselling even.' Angela helped me to gain some good perspective on my troubles, you know. I am so grateful to her."

I let out a big sigh. I have had to take in so much in the past hour or so. Faith lets out an unexpected giggle: "I am telling you Maki, some of us would not get paid if it were up to Lalang. We would be given a portion of our wages some months and other months we would have to write motivations why we deserved to be paid at all. The office gods, I tell you!"

"You reckon!" I say, smiling faintly.

"I can almost imagine her sitting on her high chair, her nose lifted even higher, as she let us in, one by one. Maphefo would go in, and her posture would change to a more welcoming one. They would immediately start talking and laughing hysterically as I nervously await my turn outside. And then she would give Maphefo her full pay plus a portion of mine. Then she would release her for the day. It is after all payday, and her dearest friend has some errands to run. And then it would be poor *Faith's* turn to get *her* paycheck.

She would put on her unwelcoming face as I enter, checking me out from top to bottom repeatedly, looking disgusted at my rather modest dress sense or maybe at the grey scent of my perfume. Then I would hand her my motivation, trembling as a servant must in front of her master. She would read the motivation with her back to me as I sit trying hard to read her head gestures in the absence of facial expressions, slowly resigning myself to the looming fact that I was not getting paid at all this month."

I cannot help but laugh, interrupting Faith's blue fantasy. But she is unfazed. And I observe her serious expression and start worrying that she either believes the story or had recounted it so many times that she was beginning to feel it strongly.

"And then she would finally look up and tell me that my motivation was not strong enough for my full pay. She would then tell me that for the month, she was not even going to afford me half my salary, but would want a list of my financial commitments so she could pay them on my behalf. And because she is kind, she would afford me a small stipend on top of that," she adds with a sadness so thick it blew my breath right back to my face, hot as a heat wave.

"What if your expenses are more than your full pay?" I ask, and without waiting for an answer, I tell her that she would not be that irresponsible anyway.

One explanation I began to afford myself about the work situation, for the sake of my sanity, was that Lalang had to sit with this vacant position for so long that she got used to not having someone in the position I'm in. Maphefo gladly stepped in, whether in reality or just perceptually.

But even I knew I was consoling myself, just as much as Faith knew. This was just how things had been happening, and whatever the bond between the two was truly about, one thing was clear – it was one hell of a bond! It was like the bond between comrades in a political party who knew where the bodies have been buried and could send the sniffer dogs out at a click of their fingers. Certain holds mean that all other senses would have to take a back seat, unfortunately.

Communication woes

A s much as Lalang said she had given up on the infightings, I still had to speak to her, again. So the next day, after
handing the situation to my maker, I go to Lalang's office
with the unwavering hope that she would assist me and
together we could get to the bottom of all the issues, and
resolve them.

But as it was the previous time, Lalang appears to me
like a defeated woman. "I tried everything. The two just
do not get along. Those two don't love each other, and
I really don't know what to do. It takes Faith too long to
grasp the work. On the other hand, this Maphefo overrates herself way too much. It's just a difficult situation,"
Lalang responds.

I can hardly stand the hypocrisy, but I manage to main-
tain a professional stature. "I believe that we are all unique
individuals with unique sets of skills that, ideally, would
complement each other. That's why we work as a team. I
might be competent at public speaking but less so at writing. As colleagues, we need to make up for one another's
weaknesses and not expose them. Love conceals, it does
not expose.

As far as the learning process is concerned, we all learn
differently. If someone is struggling to learn, it could be

that the methods used or even the physical or emotional environment they are presented with, is not conducive for that person to learn optimally. They might therefore only appear to be incompetent," I respond, hoping to get her to look at the situation differently. But she gets up and says she needs to go to Kaitlyn's office.

I leave Lalang's office with the hope that something would have sunk in. I open my emails and am greeted by an 'invitation to a workshop,' from none other than Maphefo. I quickly open the mail. The message is directed to a manager in another organisation, and the opening line suggests it was sent on Lalang's behalf. Since I am not privy to the proposed meeting and I have only been copied on the email, I have no reason to think that I had much to do with the meeting. I click on the attachment and almost fall off my chair when I see the proposed agenda. Not only am I required at this meeting, but I'm also expected, according to the agenda, to make a presentation. I also notice that Lalang would only be doing the introductory remarks and purpose of the meeting. If this is the culture in this unit, then it is way too foreign to me. Painfully foreign. Was I being a crybaby for expecting to be consulted on the agenda, at the very least? I mean let alone be part of the decision regarding the convention in the first place!

Why has no one mentioned even the need for this meeting to me? How on earth does Maphefo decide on a date without checking with me first, especially since she does not keep my diary? It is not a convenient appointment at all. I cannot be away on this day because it just so happens to fall within the two days when my husband will also be out of town. It has never happened because we both usually have some measure of control over our schedules, especially Makhananisa. Who is going to look after the kids? I fall back against my chair, feeling defeated. It's too late now to ask Makhananisa to reschedule with his clients. I had thought that dilemmas such as this one were a thing of the past because as a manager now, I would at least have more influence and control over my schedule and not be willy-nilly expected to go to out of town meetings on dates that don't suit me. Even as a middle manager in my previous organisation, I never imposed dates on people if I could help it; every meeting date and time had to suit all involved before it could be communicated externally. In this unit, however, such liberty is considered luxury. Someone else makes all the decisions on my behalf, military style. That someone at this stage appears to be either Maphefo or Lalang or the two of them together.

After giving the email some thought and allowing myself to put everything in the right perspective, I decide that my concerns need to be communicated or I would be dancing to the tunes of others all the time.

I forward the email to Lalang with a message that I would have preferred to be part of the decisions pertaining to the meeting since I'm expected to give a presentation. I have no doubt that my point is sincere and would be understood. I think that by tackling the issues early on, I would stand a good chance of setting some communication standards and of establishing courtesy rules.

I was therefore not prepared for any negative interpretation or any grave reaction to my email. My *ignorance* led me to believe that naturally, as a manager, Lalang would put herself in my shoes and immediately recognise, maybe even acknowledge that this truly was no proper way of doing things. But boy, was I wrong! I could never have anticipated the lash out that I received from Lalang.

"Maki, I know nothing about the arrangements for that meeting. I have nothing to do with matters of your component. You should stop whining and complaining and start managing your staff. This is not your previous organisation," she responds in a rather unpleasant email.

I am taken aback. Although I indeed had gotten used to a certain level of courtesy and cooperation, I never once referred to how we did things in my previous workplace. Secondly, how could Lalang say she had nothing to do with the arrangements when the email was clearly written on her behalf?

If her statement had any truth in it, then things were much worse than I had thought because it would, therefore, imply that Maphefo was the one that made decisions without so much as consulting or collaborating, neither with myself nor with Lalang. It means Maphefo was free to act on Lalang's behalf, without her knowledge, whenever she deemed it necessary.

Careful not to anger her any further, I respond by first apologising for the misunderstanding, and then I explain that it was only because the message stated that "this communique is sent on behalf of Ms Lalang Masego," that I thought she would be the right person to raise my concerns with. "I would talk to Maphefo, though," I say.

I decide to take the short walk to Maphefo's workstation instead of sending an email. Emails have a way of being misunderstood, some spirit of their own it seems. Maphefo gives me her usual 'what now?' look. She gave me the same look the day before when I walked over to her desk to hand her the employee card she had forgotten in the ladies room. She had then managed to quickly switch from the questioning look to a friendlier one when I presented the card to her but still abstained from saying a simple 'thank you.'

"Why are you not saying thank you?" I had asked her as I moved away from her station, and she surprisingly told me she had thanked me. "Oh, I must have missed that," I managed to say even as I knew for certain she had not thanked me, at least not out loud. I expected her to wear a more inviting mask today; after all, I extended some humanity to her yesterday. But she gazes at me with those huge, expressionless eyes that never seem to blink. She has eyes so big a small birdie could make an attempt to get in them, in much the same way a small insect might get into a person's eyes. If only they weren't so much without life, they would have qualified as sensual.

Since the writing was on the wall that mine was not expected to be just a friendly visit, I quickly ask Maphefo why she did not consult with me regarding the meeting. I even attempt a smile as I ask, to make my question less confrontational. "It was the boss lady who instructed me to schedule the meeting," she explains. I thank Maphefo and walk back to my office as red flags fly across my eyes from every direction. I've already lost count of the number of lies I have come across. Lies and deceptions. Just so much rust and rot. So much sticky mud under the waters.

After the startling revelation by Maphefo, I decide just to accept the situation – not so much the unsuitable date, but rather the nature of the concoctions that were brewing within the unit's walls. I check my emails. It did not take long for the other party to accept 'our' meeting as scheduled. What am I to do now? Should I go back to Lalang and tell her that I, unfortunately, would need to be close to home on the day of the scheduled meeting since there would not be anyone caring for the kids and taking them to school? Can I risk yet another destructive criticism? Am I maybe expecting too much because as a working mother, a manager, I should be having a full-time au pair or someone to take the load off my shoulders and allow me to be a manager on call? I accept that it was my choice not to have a childminder. After all, there are never any guarantees that if one had a nanny, she or he would always be there when unexpected meetings happen. The best way around these things, in my view, remains communication and compromise. What is the worst that could happen if I break the news to her? I doubt that she would bite. I decide to give it a try. I cannot take Sofia's advice to rather take leave on such days. I'm a manager, and I have to be more responsible and much more considerate of others. I believe one should do to others as one would have things done unto them. And *others* also happen to include people who are not so nice. I remind myself that I have never shied away from standing up for what's fair and best for myself.

So I put on my brave mask, not forgetting my bullet-proof vest. I will take those shots gracefully. "I should have stated this concern when I wrote her that email," I say as I start packing up documents on my desk in a delay tactic, so I don't have to take the dreaded walk to that office. I know I have to try. I should go raise my dilemma with Lalang as soon as possible. After that email, I really don't expect her to understand – so far her track record tells me I should be surprised if she understands. And she has thus far never disappointed.

My knocking on her open door only succeeds in getting her to raise her head a bit to check who was there. She immediately goes back to looking at her computer screen without as much as a 'come in.' I wasn't knocking to get a response anyway; I knocked because it's common courtesy to do so. I let myself in and pass a dutiful hello. She responds with some action on her nose, but nothing comes from her mouth. I ask if it was a bad time to budge in. She responds with a cold "you may sit." I sit down expecting her to move her eyes away from the screen towards my direction. And I start to speak when I notice that the environment was filling up with a heaviness and maybe even an awkwardness I was not prepared to be immersed in. She refrains from looking my way the entire time I'm speaking. Then she quickly swivels her chair to face me, and with her hand on her waist, Lalang reprimands me, telling me to step up to my position as a manager.

"I thought that since I had no say in the decision of the meeting date, it wouldn't be a problem if I shared my predicament with you. It has nothing to do with not stepping up. In as much as I'm expected to be available on demand, I also deserve to be treated like a human being and be let in on these matters. I doubt you would have welcomed any decision by me to schedule a meeting on your behalf without your say, or your request for that matter. Trust me, the last thing I wanted to do was come here and ask for any favours. I would not be here if I was not facing this dilemma. But I will go to Bloemfontein for the meeting, and I'll send you a draft of my presentation tomorrow morning."

I commit to the meeting without having a solution in mind and almost stumble on an extension cord on my way out of the hostile office. It somehow feels good to have tried. What's more, I'm learning more and more about the work culture each time I engage with Lalang.

I call Makhananisa. He assures me that we will find a way. He would try to reschedule his meeting, failing which we would have to ask either my sister or his if they could help with the kids for a day or so. We have never asked any of them for such favours. But what other choice do we have?

I begin with the draft presentation. I'm reluctant to go and talk to Lalang about the main purpose of the meeting and what my presentation should entail, so I connect the dots from Maphefo's email to the bare bits on the agenda and start to prepare a presentation.

As I look closely at the agenda, I notice that it might be possible for my trip to be in and out. It will still be a stretch though. I would have to wake up at 3am to catch a 6am flight to Bloemfontein, and rush to the 8:30am meeting. It's an hour-long flight, and I should make it to the meeting on time. The meeting will end at 16:30 and I will have to take the last flight out, at 19:30. I exhale. It would be hectic, but at least I would not have to burden my sister or my sister-in-law, and my husband could still make his meeting.

I make a quick call to ask him to hold off till tomorrow and not cancel his meeting just yet. But I soon realise that leaving the house that early would mean that the kids would be left on their own. I drop my head on the desk in frustration.

I never had household help or a nanny, mainly out of consideration for my husband who, given his private nature, would have a hard time adjusting to living with another person in the house who was not a family member. Though he gave me the go-ahead to find a helper, I decided to rather get someone who would only come in once a week and assist with the laundry and some cleaning. In my case, full-time help would not be a viable option because Makhananisa already does his own laundry, and he struggles to enjoy food prepared by, as he puts it, 'someone who has to cook because they have no choice.'

What assistance then would a helper be bringing if he or she was not going to take the daily cooking load off my back? I asked myself before deciding to let go of my fantasies of coming home to a freshly cleaned house and some inviting aroma from the kitchen. "I guess I will never come home to a wife," I joked as I informed Makhananisa of my decision to do without permanent household help.

It was a bitter-sweet decision as there were pros and cons to it. The disadvantages of not having help weigh on me at times, especially during times like these. Yes, it becomes stressful in situations like this one, when my work would do as it pleases with me, taking me to places I would rather not be, and at the most inopportune moments, as it freely sweeps away my freedom.

On the positive side, I am self-reliant and free from some of the stresses those with helpers tend to experience. My kids go to crèche, and I've never found myself stranded with a baby on a Monday morning, waiting for the nanny to come as I watched the clock ticking, slowly losing hope as my meeting at work starts without me. All because Auntie decided she could not come back on a Sunday evening from her weekend break. Or worse, she had decided to fire her boss without as much as a warning. Oh, how I wish I had the guts to fire my boss.

Whenever my "Madam" friends and sisters lament about disappearing items and how their domestics have become a law unto themselves, I tend to feel better about my nanny-less situation. "I would ask her to cook rice and chicken, and she would cook *Mala Mogodu* because she was craving it.

She wouldn't even consider why I asked for rice and chicken myself or the reason the tripe was in the fridge, and when I wanted it cooked," my friend Rebabedi once complained before firing her helper, Sarah. She had tolerated the unexplained hikes in the use of electricity, the disappearing groceries, the extended unauthorised leave, and Sarah's tendencies of choosing to interfere in her family time by sitting for hours watching television with the couple instead of watching in her own room. What irritated her more was that she held and controlled the remote too and made them watch endless movies of her choice!

I realise I cannot postpone till we get home to brainstorm over our dilemma. So I pick up my mobile and call Makhananisa to discuss the situation over the phone. He agrees that flying to and from Bloemfontein on the day will not make much of a difference as far as caring for the kids is concerned. "Go ahead and plan the overnight trip. I will make a plan," he assures me.

I write down my trip logistics and hand over my suggestions to Maphefo, who is, after all, the organiser. Then I go back to painstakingly preparing the presentation, and I manage to complete it on the same day and send it to Lalang for input. She gives her input, and the presentation is finalised and agreed upon a couple of days before the meeting.

It was custom in the unit for the entire team to contribute to presentations, and I had that covered too. The meeting was on a Friday, and while the rest of the team were planning to sleep over two nights before and after the meeting, I planned to sleep over for only the night before.

It's the day before we leave for Bloemfontein and all looks good and well. Makhananisa managed to reschedule his meeting, the travel arrangements have been made, and I have a final draft presentation ready. But as I prepare to go home on Wednesday afternoon, before I could say goodbye and maybe even harvest some well wishes and tips from Lalang, my phone rings.

Lalang summons me into her office. I immediately lead myself there. On her laptop screen, I notice that there is a presentation, but it's not the same one we finalised on Monday.

"I'm seriously concerned. It does not seem like we are on the same page about this project," Lalang says to the surprised and increasingly anxious me. I'm surprised and anxious because this is the same Lalang who had given my presentation – our presentation even – the thumbs up just a few days ago. I say a silent prayer and prepare my rustled nerves to handle whatever lambasting I was evidently to receive. "We are not piloting here; this is the actual evaluation, and you're going there to introduce it," says Lalang.

I find myself both relieved and shocked by the reason for Lalang's scathing remarks about not being on the same page. Her words had given me the impression that I must have made a huge mistake somewhere. Still, the so-called misunderstanding about the meeting having to do with a pilot was a shock since it was Lalang who said the purpose of the visit was to prepare to do a pilot, then an evaluation. What sort of person am I working with here?

There are so many complete lies and half-truths. Is it possible that I'm working with a liar, or a somewhat twisted persona, I ask myself as I sit there listening to every word.

Lalang had drastically changed the presentation. She had no regard for the fact that I was already prepared to deliver my presentation, having given myself enough time to understand the issues we wanted to deal with so that I do not present something I did not fully understand. But old Lalang had gone and reversed my progress. I listen as Lalang tries to summarise her new presentation and what it entails. I feel dispirited, but being one never to shy away from challenges, I take some notes and accept the presentation. After asking for some clarity on her presentation, some slides of which, according to Faith, have been repeated to the same audience for donkey years, I resolve to simply accept things as they were.

"I will spend the evening acquainting myself with the new presentation," I say as I leave Lalang's office. Then Lalang stops me and breaks the news that she was not going to make it to the meeting herself due to another engagement. I was already suspecting that she won't be coming along because she didn't seem to care about the trip arrangements at all.

Faith's words a few days ago now ring true in my ears. "She will not go, you'll see," she had predicted, but I dismissed her prophesy because I didn't have the history behind me as far as Lalang's tactics were concerned. But Faith was not imagining things it now appears; she was talking from experience since Lalang had apparently never attended any similar meetings in the past. "I've been here for more than four years now and have observed that she would keep including her name in the meeting schedules but would always find a reason not to attend the actual meeting, often dropping the team at the very last minute," Faith adds during my call to her after leaving Lalang's office. "That's her style," she says. If nothing else, it's comforting to realise that all this was at least, not about me. It had absolutely zilch to do with me as a person, and I would be doing myself a huge injustice if I did not accept that going forward.

I also have to quickly accept that not only will I be presenting a different presentation from what I prepared, but I'll be doing so without Lalang's support. I was in essence, all on my own.

The people we are visiting know nothing of these internal miscommunications; I still need to be professional and give them a good presentation. I keep reminding my spirit at short intervals when it drifts towards self-pity and strife. And then that crying voice in my head would start: *I spent the last few evenings rehearsing the presentation only to be told at the last hour to discard everything and prepare a new presentation.* The roller coaster of pain and self-counselling continues for an hour before I concede that 'such is life.'

I finally manage to keep the pain and indigestion at bay, and I spend the evening acquainting myself with the new presentation. I did, of course, indicate during my job interview that I was a quick learner, and that much is still true. I will be alright.

"I'm so happy just to be away from Lalang, even if it's just for a day," I say to Faith, almost in a self-consoling tone.

"You are breaking the promise you made to both of us not to mention that name at all today," Faith says as she slips further into the hotel's comfortable armchair to relax.

"I think the challenge is that though I try to remove it from my lips, the name is somehow always at the back of my mind. That's what makes it so difficult not to blurt it out."

"Never let her hear you say you are happy to be away. Remember she always looks for opportunities to hurt us, and she would make sure we never leave the office again if she gets the slightest idea that we may be enjoying our time out of office," Faith says with laughter, before drifting back to the self-pity lane and staying there for longer than both of us had planned.

"I don't know what you and I have ever done to Lalang, you know. I'm certain she won't be retiring until the system kicks her out because I would imagine she hates the idea of us being free of her when she retires. I bet even when she feels a bit under the weather, all that would be needed for her to kick those warm blankets would be the thought of the two of us breathing a bit easier and working in peace."

"Isn't it amazing though, Faith, that while she may be doing that, we would pull the blankets over our heads whenever we think of going to work? At least I know I do, even if it's just for another minute's stalling beneath the covers."

Faith and I call it a night after having had an impromptu but great counselling session that benefitted both of us. I go through the presentation one more time before I slip into bed. I think about Maphefo's strange behaviour at dinner. How could anyone travelling with a team of three, elect to sit by herself at a two-seater table if she wanted both of us to join her? Maybe I'm being petty, but Faith already told me about that aspect of Maphefo.

As a team leader, I thought I could do something to bring the two together, even if just for this trip. Of course, I'm required to treat Lalang's crony like glass, at whatever expense. I chose therefore not to ruffle the feathers. After all, everyone deserves to enjoy their meal in the company of people at whose sight they would not choke on their food. Let Maphefo do whatever makes her bread tastier.

* * *

I'm trying to run away, but my behind is glued to the chair, and I cannot stand. The monster has already crawled past some of the attendees on our side of the table, and past Maphefo and Faith and it was clearly coming straight at me. Its eyes are pale, and it looks as though it's about to shed its skin. It has some scales which are pointing up in a line, making it appear to be injured. When it unexpectedly howls angrily at me, I try to lift the chair from the bottom so I can run off while carrying the chair since I cannot stand, but the chair prickles my palms and blood flows, falling on the tiled floor. Faith stands up as though to assist me; she's trying to scream something at me but I cannot hear a word she is saying.

I notice Maphefo and a few of the attendees just staring blankly at me as the rest look on in terror. As it lifts its head, looking me in the eye like it had been rehearsing this intimidation strategy and knows exactly what it was doing, I scream for God's protection and wake up from the dream dripping with sweat in the middle of a cold Bloemfontein night.

I thank God that it was all merely a dream. But I cannot stop myself from analysing it and wondering about its significance. I pray that the dream stays away from me and I fall asleep again.

"You need to heighten your prayer life; we all need to. We work with serpents," Faith says as I relate the nightmare to her during breakfast. Maphefo walks past us without as much as a good morning and elects to sit by herself again at a table meant for two. She has little choice where to sit later on during lunch though, so she sits with us then.

The presentation was done and dusted. It had gone way better than expected and any criticism was on the unit as a whole and the manner in which we communicate our meetings. I know it falls more on Lalang and maybe Maphefo, so I'm not really bothered. What bothers me, though, is the fact that it was clear the person on the other side of Maphefo's lunchtime phone conversation was Lalang, and she was asking Maphefo how the presentation went.

I check my phone, which is on the table, to see if I might have missed Lalang's call. I would have expected her to check with me as the team leader instead of first contacting Maphefo. Faith and I look at each other in surprise as Maphefo excuses herself after having said: "it went okay, Madam."

"She's now going to enlighten Lalang in secret about how stupid we both are. They thrive on this kind of gossip. It's the reason Lalang would request feedback from her and not from you. She expects something juicy, and Maphefo knows that, which is why she now left the table to spice things up for her master," Faith says after having given Maphefo one nasty look as she stood up.

So much has happened since my arrival at the organisation, it feels as though I'm in some kind of a movie where the action never seems to stop. I'm starting to look at whatever happens or doesn't happen, as a witness. I'm not going to allow my heart to partake in any of these painful acts anymore. I often choose to still give Lalang the benefit of the doubt. I am relatively new, and she's not used to my presence yet, and that's why she continues to engage Maphefo and not me. I have to keep telling myself that this is the case. But I cannot fool myself. There were too many signs that things were not about to change. Faith was right. One can do nothing but pray and hope.

"She is very lucky that she gets managers who are good and hard-working. But all of them that came before you had left on lateral transfers. That should tell you something," Faith adds.

At the airport I call my mother, not to whine and whimper, but more to hear her ever so soothing voice. "What is going on, my girl? You don't sound like yourself." There's no fooling a mother ever, is there? Unlike the kind of opportunistic bond often shared between office allies such as Lalang and Maphefo, this one is genuine. It's not man-made; it comes from the heavens above. It's pure as love itself and does not thrive on gossip, threats or even self-importance.

Before I could put together a constructive sentence to relay that I would soon come home for some much-needed 'breast milk,' my mother's maternal instincts hits the nail on the head: "My child, remember my lesson from the javelin ... If you lie down after throwing, how could you expect the javelin to stay up in the air for long? Get up, my child, and fuel its energies; see it fly away!"

I tell my mother that the new job was less than perfect and instead of saying: "I told you to stay where you found your fulfilment and stop going around changing jobs; I told you to grow where you have been planted like we did in the past," she lovingly asks if I was documenting everything that was happening. Of course, I was documenting it. "You know what they say, child; if life hands you lemons, make lemonade." I thought I was already making lemonade just by staying cheerful.

But mother had a different idea. "Be the social activist that you are. You have a story right there to tell, my child. You could help a lot of people. Do not let your experience be in vain. Let it help managers everywhere to at least re-examine the way they manage and how their management styles may be negatively affecting others by disabling their potential and productivity. Better still, let those wounds make you some money. Turn your story into a blog, maybe even a book."

As we say goodbye to each other, I stand still for a moment pondering on mom's advice. Goodness, I think she may be on to something here.

6

Death by work

I don't think for a moment that when the African ancestor said that "a man dies as a result of what he eats," he'd meant it was applicable to one's work. That one's source of livelihood could be the cause of one's ultimate demise.

My long-time friend Ingrid and I had not seen each other in months. We had, however, talked endlessly on the phone about her work situation and the stresses that consumed her, courtesy of her new manager, Taelo. When Taelo joined the organisation my friend worked for, she brought along with her an entourage in the form of a new team for her office, which included an administrator – a position that Ingrid had been holding for over five years. Since there were no other vacant administrator positions in the organisational structure, something, or more specifically, someone, had to give.

For many, including Ingrid, Taelo's entry into the organisation had led to a swollen and sore season of irrational demotions, constructive dismissals, and expensive court battles. For a long time, Ingrid showed immense strength amidst an aching heart. But finally, the woeful calling of death: work woes killed Ingrid.

"Many might fall, but not this one – not Ingrid! She had come such a long way in this battle, and she was so strong!

This is just so wrong; it's too painful!" Our friend Rebabedi's cries hover in the air, piercing at the spirit.

She and Ingrid lived a street away from each other, and they had spent many cosy Saturday afternoons together – many hours in which they talked, cried, prayed, laughed and drew from each other the strength to keep moving. They kept fighting the workplace demons that were after Ingrid's livelihood, and in a lot of ways, after the blood running through her veins and the very air she breathed.

The two friends had spent many hours during which they both learnt of true faith and resilience. The rest of us made it a point of meeting once a quarter as a group. While we're envious of the time that Rebabedi was able to spend with Ingrid, we also realise how much more intense the shock hit her.

They were together the very Sunday afternoon before she suddenly passed on only two hours after they had said their cheerful goodbyes. It was a shock as we all so strongly believed that victory was inevitable. If anyone could win a fight like this, it was going to be Ingrid, we thought.

As we sit together as a handful of Ingrid's friends, sobbing and ruminating over whatever subtle clues we think our friend might have given us which might have signalled to us that we either needed to give her more support, or maybe, look at her much more intensely and take in her essence to keep us company as we continued on this journey, we all agree on one thing: people like Ingrid simply did not die. Her unwavering spirit, melodic voice, cheerful nature, and a myriad of creative skills all could not be wasted in a lonely, cold grave. We take comfort in the sense we all have that all of her gifts would live on, not just with us, but into eternity.

We also agree that when we often tell ourselves that we don't have time to visit and spend time with one another, we lie to ourselves as human beings. My mind clogs with all the missed opportunities to meet for a cuppa. They fly across my face as though I was watching flashes of my life in probably the same way people say they experience in the face of death. I should have passed by her house after work sometime. "Look at us now.

Upon hearing the devastating news of Ingrid's passing, we all couldn't care less about what our bosses would say as we hurriedly put aside the forever urgent reports, left our respective workplaces and headed for Ingrid's house. We had suddenly turned our backs on other plans because this was way too important. This was about the very depths of life itself. How could we not be here? How could any of us claim to be too busy when the real matters of life and death have stepped in?

Suddenly nothing else could be more important now that our friend is no more. Our families could wait, just this once. If only we could make up our busy minds to give just half the attention to living, to loving and caring for one another, as we do to death," I say in response to the torments playing on my mind's rewind button. Today, we couldn't care less what our children are fed for dinner because we know that even if it so happened that they'd miss a meal, it wouldn't be enough to kill them. Ingrid's children were now without a mother.

We will all be gathered here again on Saturday to pay our last respects and give our dear friend a loving send off. We will all be present, with our earlier excuses about how busy we would be to meet on that same Saturday haunting us.

What happened to all the very important reasons we gave for our unavailability this weekend? We've now laid aside all the reasons we gave for not keeping to our quarterly get-together. We'll be laying our friend to rest on that very day we were supposed to meet as friends, but resolved we couldn't. We have deluded ourselves when we said we were all committed. But we are now suddenly available for the funeral because we realise that nothing transcends life and death. Absolutely nothing! Not our jobs, and certainly not any home-cooked dinners. Nor the pain we derive from our over-analysis of daily occurrences that lead to misjudgements and disagreements.

Managers can kill. They might have no tangible power or will to do it physically, but the emotional and intellectual abuses at work are capable of becoming like cancerous growths that feed on the daily little cruelties they are made of and grow into monstrous killers. Bullies, particularly bully employers, must never deceive themselves – most have murdered one way or another. They create enormous stress for their victims and bully them to their early graves. They carry on with their business, hiding behind tales of 'unexplained' sudden deaths. What sort of monsters would be housed inside a person's core for them to derive even the slightest pleasure and delight over another's anguish?

"Just show me one grave of someone that died from hunger," my former colleague, Nkele, responded as we gathered around her in an effort to get her to reconsider her impulsive decision to resign a few years ago.

She had surprised everyone with a resignation that Monday morning, and with no clear income plan, we thought she was making a huge mistake and throwing her family into a possible poverty pit that could take generations to correct.

The stress she felt at work has been felt deeply only by her. Our awareness of what unreasonable pressures her manager put her under, and the words of encouragement we shared with her, had finally waned. She would rather be out of a job and die of hunger than stay in a job and die of stress – except, as far as she was concerned, the former would not kill her.

She believed that even amidst the poverty we witnessed daily, we likely didn't know of any single person that starved to death. At least not one person whose grave we could identify. That is why Nkele had dared us to show her the evidence – "not many graves at all; show me just one." Sure people have died of hunger, but hunger's grave none of us could present. But work's grave I, for one, was now seeing.

We gather again at Ingrid's funeral, together in deep grief. We all vow not to let Ingrid's passing be in vain. We will support her family as best we can, and will expose the causes of Ingrid's death. Most importantly, we will be better managers, and better colleagues and friends ourselves. We will never again let our natural talents and gifts lie dormant. We will use them for the betterment of the human race because that's the reason we've been given various talents. And most of all, we will not take for granted the accumulating power the little everyday stresses have to weigh us down.

And so it is that one Tuesday morning in November I step into the psychiatrist's office, having been referred by the company contracted to offer counselling services at work. I certainly could not take the stress anymore.

"Very few people get counselling for work-related stress, even as so many employers offer free professional counselling to their employees. People just don't realise how much the pain eats at their quality of life. I'm glad you're taking this step to see me." Dr Bolele says when she finally opens her mouth after allowing me to shed a river of tears as I explain my work life problems and the many health issues that have recently been paying me unannounced visits.

"I should have used the window period and reversed my decision to join the organisation. I should have gone back early on because it really did not take long before I saw Lalang's colours," I say regretfully. "But I told myself that running away from life's little nuisances was just not in my nature. I joined the organisation for a reason, and I wanted to complete what I started. This is also why, up to this point, I've stood my ground and vowed only to leave when I was ready to, not because I was being pushed to leave."

"Tell me more about the anxiety you say you have recently been experiencing," she sneaks her question in the moment I finish blowing my nostrils.

"Certainly, Doctor. I might be mistaken, but I've identified the sinking unhappiness I feel every morning as I prepare to go to work as anxiety. My work has become agonisingly unpredictable and every morning as I drive to work my mind drives itself to all sorts of places as it tries to prepare for the unknown that could, in all likelihood await in that inbox.

The ghosts at night have developed a tendency to deliver, at the darkest hour, messages about everything ranging from a meeting that I'm supposed to attend urgently, which would have been known by the sender for days if not weeks, to random attacks about how the unit is underperforming and how less of a team we are. These are all pinned to me even though I found the problems there.

Whenever I think of where I'm heading, my stomach would curl, and I would take gasps and deep breaths as I attempt to stop my head from getting foggy in traffic. Walking into the unknown Monday to Friday, and doing it again and again, is slowly turning me into a bundle of nerves and is clogging my creativity and innovativeness. I feel as though my brain has been switched off."

"Have you attempted to resolve the situation, in any way?"

"I have, Doctor. I started by giving the relationships with my manager and subordinates a chance to settle as I believed the wars to be teething problems. I understood that we needed to find each other as a unit, and appreciate our different working and management styles. I knew that as the weeds got untangled and the thorns burnt, there would be pain.

We could not avoid clashes, and some level of discomfort as each one of us would be guarding our zones. But I noticed that instead of things getting better, they were actually worsening. I then decided to confront the situation differently by giving to my manager as good as she gave to me. I told myself this was a game which two could play, and I started returning the verbal blows. My retaliatory blows were met equally with further blows. I stepped right into Lalang's turf, and my frustrations led me to her trap so she could devour me.

"I have heard, Doctor, that sometimes life would present us with exactly the experiences we need for our advancement and growth. But I struggle to believe any good ever comes from immense suffering. How does pain ever help anyone? Why would the universe not make our learning less painful?"

"How do labour pains ever help anyone? Has any good ever come out of labour pains? Any at all?" the doctor responds with questions of her own.

"I hear you. But I'm not stubborn in any way, and I'm receptive enough to learn even from the softest of prickles. Why would the universe still allow situations such as the one I find myself in?" I respond and follow up with a little internal prayer. *'Lord please, if you ever feel that you have to teach me anything, please, please do it gently. And Lord, if I ever seem not to have opened my senses to your gentle touch or whisper, will you gently force them open, please Lord? I believe myself to have been made gentle, and I believe*

I'm a sensible person and will never deliberately choose to not heed your advice,' I say inwardly, looking up and with my hands in a praying mode.

The doctor doesn't interrupt me. She seems to have been with me in my prayer because as soon as I finish, she starts talking. She must have been reading my body language.

"I don't want to enforce my beliefs on you, but I will say what I believe would help you. No situation is ever permanent; we're always evolving, and everything around us changes eventually. So every situation, no matter how deep-rooted it seems, will change. All earthly kingdoms will end. Have the tough and rooted walls of certain famous places not come tumbling down one historic day? Even your troubles will end. Sometimes it seems as though nothing is happening, but I assure you without our interference, the world keeps moving and things happen every second that we could never comprehend."

"What about karma? Where is she when one needs her most?" I ask.

"Things happen at the right time, when we are ready for them to happen. They might not happen when we want them to, but when they do happen, you will know it is the right time. You were right to attribute certain problems to teething problems. There is a phase in team development called 'storming' where boundaries get pushed, and there is a lot of conflict. It is too early to determine if the team has failed. We should hope that norms will be established after this uncomfortable phase and that things will get better for you.

"This is not to say we will not be managing your situation. We'll end this session with you writing a short test," she says, showing me a questionnaire. You are to answer as honestly as you can. It will assist me in giving you the right diagnosis, support, and treatment. It will take about half an hour."

The doctor takes a deep breath, as though on my behalf or to signal to me that it was what I needed to do. Aromatherapy oils. I could do with some inhalation every now and then. I smile and set out to answer the multiple choice questions that make up the assessment.

7

Expensive tastes and earth-shattering shoes

"Explain to me, my love, those shoes that cost so much money, how would they respond to a pile of crap on the road? I certainly would understand if they have sensors and would cause any crap in their way to vibrate and move aside, so they won't step in it like any cheap shoe," Makhanisa says to me on seeing the price tag of the new pair I had just afforded myself.

I respond with a laugh to the sarcastic question. He never runs out of remarks whenever something he considers ridiculously costly is on the table. Once he asked a shop attendant who was pitching a beautiful, yet pricey handbag I admired, "Sister, this handbag, this superior, high-flying handbag you're enthusiastically describing to my wife, you reckon it has abilities that other less pricey handbags don't have, such as being able to transport us from this point and deposit us safely and comfortably at our home?"

He always had a cutting question to ask of anything he considered unreasonably priced. But he knows I'm no spendthrift by any means, so we both know it's all meant in jest.

Through years of living together, I've come to appreciate his in-depth price analysis. My extravagant friend,

Sofia, is always the recipient of my attempts at channelling my husband's sarcasm where money is concerned. So when Sofia calls me one day to pass by her home after work and see her recent purchase, which she describes as shiny and stunning and would potentially be life-changing for her, I quickly ask Makhananisa to pick up the kids so I could go and congratulate Sofia on her new, shiny purchase, which from what I could gather, was probably a new set of wheels. It was about time Sofia afforded herself some independence and stopped calling cabs for the most trivial of trips.

Though excited in anticipation of the purchase, I worry about affordability. Sofia is way too excessive, with a poor credit record to boot. She lives alone in a rented place and has nothing in the way of assets.

My attempts at getting her to invest in at least a property she could call her own had fallen so many times on deaf ears that I'd resolved to accepting that it was okay for her to live like that since she had no beneficiaries who would ultimately suffer the consequences of any poor decisions. She hadn't been tasked with parenting responsibilities so *she* lived a carefree lifestyle, I consoled myself.

After coming out of the rush hour traffic in one piece, I park my car in Sofia's empty carport. I'm glad someone didn't decide to loan the space for free today, I think to myself. Obviously, Sofia would not park her new wheels here if she wanted to introduce *her* to me herself. "Oh hi, babes, so glad you're here." I didn't expect to hear her larger-than-life voice already. Was she looking out the window waiting for my arrival or what! She couldn't have known I was here because she had given me an access code two hours ago already.

"Hello there! You look good ... sorry, I mean gorgeous, exquisite!"

"Oh, we certainly are making some progress I see, darling — no more weather or weight-related greetings. I am so glad! I can retire now."

"How are you though, Sofs?"

"Me - well, I'm cooking on gas, baby; I am cooking on gas! How was your drive?"

"The traffic was a bit hectic, as always. And I almost got into some road rage situation after flashing my lights at a car in front of me," I say using my hands to signal to Sofia that it was just one of those things that we shouldn't waste time on.

"Oh, did someone throw litter out of their window? I told you to stop flashing lights at people like that. You will never change their disgusting behaviour," Sofia scolds me, guessing correctly what might have happened and finishing off the story I was reluctant to finish off myself.

She was right; maybe I needed to stop trying to reprimand people because the only thing my actions seem to achieve is more litterbugs irritating me with their uncultured habit. I seem to attract more and more of them. But what if the universe was making sure I regularly came in contact with litterers simply because my reprimands were actually working and making some difference?

"It really baffles the mind how anyone thinks that while they cannot stand dirt in their cars, the rest of us have to deal with their filth on our roads. It looks like classic selfishness to me, and that's why I make sure to signal their unpleasant behaviour to them. Hopefully, someone takes the lesson."

I don't think I've ever spoken this long without Sofia interrupting. She was, after all, the talkative one. But I cannot help being distracted by Sofia's unusually long lashes. I'm used more to the classier style with shorter fakes, not the hairy things she was flashing that looked like some wild

Mopani worms preparing for unprecedented cold weather in summer!

"Are you absolutely sure you are okay though, my friend?" I ask staring at her lashes, almost missing a step in the process.

"What's wrong with you? Have you ever seen me pretending to be okay when I'm not? Actually, have you ever seen me in a bad mood?"

"There's nothing wrong with your behaviour or mood, dearie. It's just those lashes you are flashing. I always view them as though they are distracters, like people hide behind them, and you have never before gone that haywire, have you? They somehow seem to be hiding some tears, and I'm a little worried. Besides, I'm not used to you keeping quiet for such long periods as I waffle away."

She bursts out laughing. "The only tears I may possibly be hiding would have to be from the onions I was chopping just now, my friend, because I am making you a nice warm, soulful soup." I'm pleasantly surprised because if I was ever to expect any eats from Sofia's pad, it would be something made by someone else for Sofia's keen microwave oven. But I'm ready to be her taster because I can bet my last cent this was the first time she ever made soup.

As we enter her flat, I'm greeted by a beautiful sight of silver and red pots on her stovetop. These were obviously not here the last time I came. Before I could say something about the pots, Sofia is already in presentation mode, showing them off.

"Here we are, this right here is what brings you here this evening — my newly acquired miracle pots. They cost me an arm and a leg darling, and you would know what I would have preferred them to cost me, right?" she says laughing as she ushers me towards her new gourmet collection and the utensils for the soup she was making. "I couldn't get you here to show you empty pots, my dearie. Even I know that would be a flagrant sin."

"Wow, miracle pots, you say! Please excuse my party-pooping, but Sofia, may I remind you that you do not cook! Are these pots going to miraculously turn you into a gourmet chef? No wait, are they actually going to discourage your boxed dinners?" I quickly realise I was acting like my husband and before Sofia's frown could come full circle, I turn my words around and spice them with a dramatic: "What's in these beauties sure smells good! I mean, what a marvel your pots are, Sofs!" And they truly were beautiful.

Her phone rings just as we prepare to sit down and I'm not sure she heard my compliment. I can immediately tell she's talking to one of the transgender kids she gives moral support to. She wasn't going to tell her to call later. No, not this one, not this matter. Not even if her soup was at risk of burning and ruining her awesome new pots.

My friend Sofia was born Sol. *He* is undergoing a very complicated, demanding and expensive medical procedure to have his sex changed. *He* always rubbishes the advice that I sometimes give to *him* that *he* should rather opt for a less expensive, if not totally free, option involving simply getting himself bitten by a crab. Though nobody was ever recorded as having experienced sex change this way, it was a general belief that we held growing up. This myth was probably created as a way of discouraging behaviour that was regarded as homosexual, as no kid wanted to hear the words "if you keep doing that act, we will quickly assist you by taking you to the river and get you bitten by a crab so you can change to a boy, or a girl," – depending on the kid's gender.

I leap off the sofa at the thought of being bitten by a crab as my mind drifts to a couple of years ago during a holiday at the beach when I had felt something quivering under my left bun. I had checked casually, not expecting to see something that was believed to be holding miraculous powers to change even a girly girl like me into a boy. I jumped the same way then. I love being a girl too much. Periods, labour pains and everything considered, I would still choose to be a girl. So any crabby experiments should rather be taken by Sofia.

I laugh at myself for being a victim of my own ideas. I'm lucky Sofia did not notice. She always gives her young transgender friends her undivided attention. She's so passionate about helping others like her who've had to live their lives feeling like they were trapped in wrong bodies. She particularly supported school children who felt judged and unaccepted, both by their peers and teachers.

As she hangs up, she exclaims loudly: "Seriously Maki, what does gender have to do with a child's right to education? What on earth do these school principals want with what could be inside a kid's pants? I can understand kids being ignorant and nasty, but adults, really!"

"What's wrong, Sofia; was that Fhulu?"

"Yes, and guess what? The school principal refuses for her to wear a dungaree because, for whatever reason, he thinks he understands Fhulu's gender better than Fhulu *herself*. He says *she* is a boy. I just cannot, for the life of me, grasp what is so difficult for people to understand about being born in the wrong body. If we can understand that a child born with three legs is, for lack of a better word, nature's mistake, why can't we comprehend that it's possible for a child to be born with a private part which their whole being struggles to identify with?

I think we have to advocate for a society in which gender is not defined at birth, but defined at a certain age by an individual. It's a pity because doctors can immediately see when, for example, a new baby is having a parasitic twin that needs to be removed, but they have no way of knowing at birth that that willy should not have been."

"I don't claim to comprehend these transgender issues my friend, but what I see you doing is supporting children in distress, and that in itself is a great job, Sofs. I've heard of some children even taking their own lives because of the pressure and non-acceptance by society and often by their own families. I just cannot imagine what life would have been like if I was not accepting of my gender as a girl. So if your lending an ear and a hand could mean the difference between life and death for them, then you're making an immeasurable contribution here," I respond.

Sofia manages to let out a giggle. "You, Maki, I'm so in awe of you, you know. I should appreciate you more than I do, seriously. The normal reaction people like us get, particularly from people of your faith is that we are de-mon-possessed for identifying with the opposite gender to what God gave us. They pray for us and refuse to accept that we have been made this way. How did you get to be so accepting and so daring to befriend the 'demon-possessed' spirit that, to some people, I am? What would your fellow churchgoers and your pastors think of you when one day they find out who your bestie is? Will you not be labelled the devil's advocate?" Sofia asks with more giggles, that weren't really giggles.

"Sofs, my acceptance and deemed support does not mean I approve or even understand. And I can neither confirm you are demon-possessed or that you are not. I am no judge."

"You sound like a politician now, my friend," Sofia says laughing.

"We interpret things differently as people of faith, Sofia. My understanding is that love is all-embracing, non-judg-mental and considerate. Even if what you have done and what you are still doing was wrong, the God I know would never shun you and would embrace you when you repent. Who am I therefore to shun you? I am not qualified to judge. The truth is, I cannot imagine you or Fhulu or many other like you electing to reject the gender you were born with just so you could be controversial and be criticised and shunned. There has to be more to this than us humans can comprehend. Some things are not earthly terrain."

"Thank goodness for your gift of empathy, Maki."

"And I do not give a hoot what fellow worshippers may think of my stance on these matters. I seek first to understand, at least I try to. I mean, who am I under the sun to evaluate such complicated issues? Who are we all to judge? My understanding of what happens at physiological and neurological levels for someone to end up forming one body part instead of the other, is way too limited for me to pass any sort of judgement. Anyway, don't they say we all start out as girls?"

"I think you're wearing the Ntsobe hat today Maki, aren't you?" Sofia laughs as she poses the rhetorical question. "You're right; we don't possess enough intelligence to decide over these matters. I've told you before that you're truly an undercover angel."

"Believe me, I know. I've finished more fights than I've founded." We laugh, with Sofia wrapping up her bit with her usual choke-like sound that often rewinds my own laughter.

"But seriously, I admire your vernacular, Maki, for not containing the words 'her or him.' That is totally progressive, doll. I respect the African ancestor for having had the spiritual intelligence and lack of gender discrimination to comprehend the significance and weight in these words. Oh, I forget we don't have the luxury of this entire evening. Tell me what is going on at work before Makhananisa innocently calls to check on you, and you start racing to the door. How is that buffoon of a manager of yours? What balls is she playing these days?"

"Oh that one, I think we need to attend to your pots first, and then I'll tell you all about her latest shenanigans. Did you hear my compliment earlier, though? The pots are stunning! They truly must have cost an arm and a leg!"

"Thank you, doll; I knew you'd love them. To be honest, they actually cost a whole lot more, my darling. I won't tell you exactly how much yet. I want to avoid that lecture of cooking from the heart on your Hart pots. But I do promise to make the purchase worthwhile. I will cook you something much more exquisite and delicious the next time you are here just so you can see this is indeed a good investment in my health. For now, it would be the soup as a starter. The main course would be on your next visit." We laugh.

Heavens know Sofia should not be buying such unnecessary things as pots because she cannot even cook rice, let alone boil an egg. What else heaven knows is that I enjoy relating Ms Lalang's stories to Sofia. I can never get over how wide her mouth opens and just how far she always has to walk to pick up her jaw because it sure doesn't drop down and stay put; it tumbles away whenever she hears the incredibly ridiculous tales of one Ms Lalang Masego. But more significantly, my friend's comments and words of encouragement not only make me laugh but give me a good dose of strength to wake up and face that cracked woman another day, until the next time we talk.

Whenever I need a shoulder to cry on or when I need to quickly pluck up the courage to deal with my annoying so-called boss, I would channel Sofia, and she never disappoints. I tell her I channel Ntsobe, but Ntsobe is really not my alter ego; as far as I am concerned, the real Ntsobe is none other than Sofia herself. She tells it like it is, with steam. Sofia, Faith, Rebabedi, my siblings, my mother, my kids, and my loving husband are mutually responsible for my sanity amidst my challenges at work. Such a support system could mean the difference between sanity and insanity, or life and death. So many workers fall into depression, so many commit suicide because of work-related stress, perhaps exacerbated by insufficient or non-existent moral support.

Work monsters are real creatures, and no one knows that better than myself. So any visit to view some expensive, colourful gourmet pots while getting a dose of Sofia's infectious laugh are absolute necessities in my world. Thank goodness Sofia is her own boss and she's stress-free enough, at least as far as work is concerned, to support and counsel me. She's a much-appreciated vessel for all my cares. She does her passion – health and beauty – for a living and her positive energy is second to none. My mother loves to say that when one does something one enjoys, there's never a shortage of positive, creative energy. I'm not sure though, whether she sees any irony in the fact that she didn't allow me to pursue my love for art, and had said that art was something I could do alongside my real job. My real, stress-infested job.

"My friend, witchcraft is by no means confined to the use of dark concoctions, poison or mysterious powers. Witchcraft is also expressed through wicked hearts, I tell you, Sofs. It must be the very reason why God searches our hearts more," I say as an introduction to what transpired since Sofia and I last spoke.

"These days I even avoid walking too close to the edge of the staircase at work lest that hateful woman blows me down the floors with just her coarse air."

I shake as Sofia unexpectedly belts out a loud laugh. I'm shaken because my mind had briefly left Sofia's flat and had travelled to the office, imagining the very scenario I was relating. I had forgotten to cushion myself for Sofia's possible reaction.

I start to feel the pain and the frustration I felt yesterday morning as Lalang completely chose to twist my words around when I said we didn't understand something the same way. That, to her, meant I was saying she was the one who didn't understand, and as a result, she later came up with an excuse why I could not be the one attending a particular workshop. Her bestie, Maphefo, would now be attending, as always.

What she didn't know was that I never wanted to go to that workshop in the first place, because I had been to one of those at my previous employer. The only reason I had not turned down her invite was that it was the first time an invite was extended to me. Rebabedi and I had already planned to go out for lunch on the day of the workshop, and I was happy to let Maphefo take it, though it would have been nice if she had given it to Faith instead, or some of the other colleagues. As she thought she was punishing me, I was rejoicing because my prayers had been answered.

I jump right on to the next story: "You won't believe how she treated me last month when I sprained my ankle and was booked off for two weeks. Remember I told you she never responds to my messages and she often claims not to have received them?

"I remember that her phone is quite selective when it comes to your messages," Sofia says as she stands up to check on the soup.

"Yes, the only messages she receives from me are responses to her own messages about work when she's out of the office and needs me to do something for her. When I'm stuck in traffic and running late, or running late for whatever other reason, and when I cannot make it work because of my own or a family member's ill health, Lalang's phone acts all nasty and deletes my messages before she reads them."

"It does exactly what she would want it to do. Nasty like the owner. And I remember that one time when you got sick of her claims not to have received your messages and you deliberately didn't send her that sick notification and claimed to have sent it," Sofia laughs.

"Yes, it was Ntsobe or maybe you who gave me the idea," I say laughing. "Remember I told you how much different and assured her anger at not having been informed was? I wish I had a camera for that moment when she got beaten at her own foolish game."

"So carry on, tell me what happened when you and your ankle were recovering."

"At the end of my first week off, Lalang called."

'Hello, how are you?' she asked.

'I'm getting better, but it's still...'

'Actually, I didn't call to ask you about that. I need that assessment report on my desk by Monday; Kaitlyn wants it as in yesterday,' she interrupted my response, making it clear she couldn't have cared less about my recovery, much to my shock. She even coats her insensitive demands with her favourite overlay – her manager Kaitlyn, whose name she often uses as the office bogeyman. And when it suits her, she also uses the same name as either a scapegoat or a ladder when around executive figures.

No wonder poor Kaitlyn has been complaining of exhaustion lately; she's being trampled on and then dragged through all manner of things."

"Does she still shock you though, girlfriend? And why didn't you tell me about this? I know just how upset she can make you feel."

"I didn't tell you because I chose not to stress you that week. Remember, it was when Kitty was ill. I have to save you sometimes, my friend. I often choose not to tell even Makhananisa about certain occurrences at work that I know would probably stress him out and make him imagine going there himself to sort out some people. Sometimes I would rather just carry things myself because there's just so much to cry about that it's easy for one to feel like a crybaby."

"Be assured, Maki. I know you're a strong woman, girl. A far cry from a crybaby! Here," she hands me a bowl of her steaming hot soup. It smells heavenly, and I pray it tastes at least half as good.

"I know, Sofs. You don't know that woman, hey. Lalang is so cold that if you needed an air conditioner on a very hot day and she entered, I promise you would suddenly reach for a heater and start unbundling all your packed fleece blankets. Even when my kids or Faith's are sick, she never seems to care. She always responds as though she doesn't trust us. Both of us have come to realise that the only reason she doesn't trust us is because she lies about being sick herself. People who are trustworthy do not typically mistrust without any reason. And I always have to kick myself for always giving her the benefit of the doubt. So she never stops shocking me, in a way. She's unbelievable ... She's like pain – no one ever gets used to how deeper it can go.

"And yesterday Maphefo was busy running around with a contribution list for Lalang's birthday next Friday, and we were all asked to make contributions towards a cake, drinks and a gift. Both of them never gave a damn about the baby shower we were arranging for our previous administrator, Kganya. And I've noticed they never make the usual financial contributions we make to colleagues during either bereavements or farewells.

"When Maphefo came with the list, Faith pretended not to be aware of Lalang's birthday. She was like 'oh, is her birthday approaching?' Faith had been there last week when during the staff meeting Lalang had bragged about sharing her birthday week with a celebrated musician. Not only was Faith present, but she didn't miss out on that opportunity to roll her eyes at the faint association to a celebrity."

"And you? Did you contribute?" Sofia asks, her body language making it clear she wasn't expecting me to have done so. She wouldn't know for sure, though, because I sometimes get absorbed into 'turning the other cheek.' But had I contributed, Sofia's piercing gaze might just have made me change my answer.

"My birthday was just a month ago, and I received nothing, Sofia. Not even a Happy Birthday message. Of course, I didn't contribute. I asked Maphefo if we were setting new standards by beginning to make financial contributions for one another's birthdays. I tell you, ever since I started working with Lalang, I've never received any form of courtesy, let alone anything closely resembling a gift. Why should I contribute my children's pocket money for someone so undeserving? Makhananisa would never have forgiven me."

"I'm so proud of you, babes! Good on you! I promise I was going to flip if you'd said you contributed. I know deep down you would like to forgive and turn the other cheek, but I'm glad for these moments when you realise you cannot forgive these people till kingdom comes. That calls for a bubbly, doesn't it?" Sofia says as she stands up to pour a drink.

"I don't know what's possessing that poor woman, but I would bet my last coin whoever bewitched her has long died because surely they would have seen the awful effects of their evil deed, pitied her and undone their spell on her. How one person can house so many demons is beyond me. It is lies, cold-heartedness, gossip, undermining others, self-importance, backstabbing, competing, jealousy, hypocrisy, sneakiness, and overall just vile and evil behaviour. Oh, did I mention two-tongued?"

"You forgot downright unsightliness!" Sofia adds with a disgusted face. We would normally have both laughed at Sofia's comment, but neither of us do. I guess the atmosphere was too laden with po-faced airs. With none of us particularly humoured, I open my mouth to explain the recent event on my mind, the very one that just evoked intense emotions and the most unsavoury descriptive words. But Sofia jumps in as I begin to talk; apparently she was not yet done with Lalang's looks. "You know, she should be grateful you didn't take after that great-grandmother of yours. Otherwise, you'd be throwing vomit at her all the time."

We laugh. "I'm ever so glad I did not inherit that from gran Modipadi. I cannot even begin to have a handle on how exactly one starts off to get nauseated by ugly people to the point of vomiting when one lay eyes on them! I know you find this amusing, my friend, but I don't; I struggle to. It baffles the mind really. Does beauty not lie in the eye of the beholder? Who qualified in my great-gran's sight as ugly, and who didn't? Who would have vomited at her sight had they suffered from the same illness as her? I mean with all respect to her memory, she did not exactly turn any heads herself!

And for the record, Lalang is not really ugly; at least I don't think she is. As far as I'm concerned, she just happens to miss her turns to smile, and she misses those quite too often. Add her stony heart to that, and she easily assumes a somewhat uglier existence. I wish she could know that her austere spirit makes her unattractive."

I shelve Sofia's insistence about Lalang's ugliness and continue with my story. "Faith had a bout of flu at the beginning of the week, and she was clearly badly struck on Monday when she apparently dragged herself to work just so Lalang could see that she was truly sick and not, in fact, suffering from a hangover. Having coughed and sneezed her way through Monday, she went to see the doctor the next day and was booked off work for the rest of the week.

But she made a mistake of calling instead of texting Lalang. I don't know why she likes to call her instead of sending a text message, because experience would have taught her that such calls would be taken without empathy and get well wishes. Instead, Lalang would complain about how bad the workload was."

"Maybe she doesn't want to deal with claims of undelivered messages," Sofia remarks dryly, referring to my usual experience when I text Lalang.

"No dear, it's my texts that Ms Masego's phone has trouble receiving. Only mine," we laugh.

"When Faith called her, true to her nature and as though she had not seen how sick Faith was the previous day, Lalang started to complain about how much work we had at the office and that Faith was behind on her work. Lalang told Faith to actually come to the office. Faith heeded the call against doctor's orders and dragged herself to the office the next day.

We were having a staff meeting, and as would be expected of someone with the flu, Faith sneezed and coughed and what not. Her eyes were as red as blood. Now, guess what! I'm not sure whether it was truly out of pity or just out of irritation at Faith's constant wheezes, but Lalang, with the most merciful of tones, suddenly goes: 'Faith my dear, you are really sick, you know, and you're going to make all of us sick in here. You should go home. You cannot go on like this'.

"I tell you I figuratively had my mouth wide open through the rest of the meeting. And I never located my jaw ever since that meeting, Sofia. I could hardly believe my ears. Her body language claimed innocence and anyone who didn't know the whole story would have given

Lalang some points in the category of empathetic manager. Nothing in her voice gave away the sad truth that Faith was at work precisely because of Doctor Lalang's orders. But then Faith refused to go home and responded with a simple 'I will be okay.'

"To be honest, I wasn't pleased with Faith for having jumped at the click of Lalang's fingers like that when she was terribly ill. After the meeting, I told Faith just how much worse she was making the situation for all of us by succumbing to Lalang's summons when both her body and her doctor had ordered her to rest. There's not a thing she could ever do to be written in Lalang's book of favourites, and she knows that. Why on earth was she bending over in all directions, paying no attention to the only body she will ever have, in the name of appeasing the unappeasable?

"'Lalang will never pause,' I'd said in my attempt to drive the message home to Faith. 'She will keep on trying to control us as long as she sees her tactics working. By dragging your ill body to this office today, you've reinforced in Lalang's psyche the absurd belief that she holds more power over us than our maker. You need to put on your big-girl panties and stand your ground sometimes. Lord knows we have given Lalang more respect than she deserves from us. We cannot give her any more without putting our well-being at risk.

Get it into your head, please: Lalang will not care if you become bed-ridden as a result of having heeded her call to come to the office. By tomorrow she would have forgotten that act she put on this morning, and she would call you back again. Shelve the peri-peri, sister, and take care of yourself'.

"Faith could not have agreed more. She had already thought about this and said she would never give Lalang that much power over her existence again. It was also for Lalang's own good in a way, I believe. Imagine if one day someone is forced to come to work in bad health, and then they drop down and die on her watch and command! What would she say having ordered the person to come to work despite what the doctor would have advised? We need to save that woman from herself and that we can do by standing firm when we know we are right.

Maybe we have been put in these challenging positions to assist her soul to grow in this area, and we would have failed if all we did was painfully endure, without ever altering here, and rerouting there."

Sofia remains in deep thought, dumbfounded I suppose. The sound of my phone cuts through the silence as it lets out a rather healing melody, and I reach for it from my back pocket. I cannot believe I've been sitting on it, yet it can still ring under so much pressure. It's like me; I still can be joyful in spite of Lalang.

I notice as I put the bowl down that I had actually been eating Sofia's debut soup all along, but I cannot recall how it tasted. I will have time to beat myself up about that later.

For now, Makhananisa is on the line. True to his nature, he has called to check if I was still fine. His care-driven calls have cut short many meetings between Sofia and I; they just seem to do that effortlessly, with no particular demands. Though he insists he only calls to check if I was still fine where I was, his calls never fail to remind me that I should be making my way home sometime on the same night and that the streets, unfortunately, are not always a safe place to be, especially at night.

At that moment I feel sorry for my husband as I comprehend his untold, manly fears. What would he say to my family if, God forbid, anything should happen to me on those streets. I feel that pain even as I imagine his family having to utter that dreaded phrase to mine – the one that simply yet profoundly states 'we have failed to shepherd.'

It wouldn't have mattered whether it would have truly been a failure on their part or not. No, they've accepted that responsibility the day I assumed their last name.

Sofia and I whimper over a tight hug as our short visit come to an end, and I thank her for the 'warm and wonderful' soup, the taste of which happens to have leaked from my mind. What she does not know would not hurt her now, would it?

I feel lighter as I prepare to drive off, attempting in vain to blow back to my friend as many kisses as *she* was blowing my way. I know *her* intention is to give me enough to continue making my lemonades. But I'm by no means a close match to Sofia as far as blowing the most kisses in the shortest time would go. A kiss blown back to *her* for every two I caught was good enough.

I'm reflecting on Sofia's words already as I drive off and I know I will be doing so for days to come: "It's only a matter of time before Lalang's true nature is uncovered. No one can hide underneath the clouds' shadows forever. She may deceive people now with her sweet tongue, but her cover will soon be blown, and she will be seen for the venomous snake that she is".

I take off my hoodie to uncover my ears so that I can see clearly through the traffic. Even I have to laugh at the irony of this act. But it's true; and I often find myself having to remove my sunglasses so I could hear the music better, or reduce the volume on the television set so I could savour the dark, sweet corners of my favourite chocolate without the other senses all vying for my undivided attention.

The memories of my short visit to Sofia become the perfect company. I do not find myself wondering about the shadows I was seeing at the back seat of my car.

Arguing with my mind when it attempted to assure me that those were, in fact, normal shadows from the beautiful jacaranda trees that kept the streets company, night and day.

I soon find myself home without ever having had time to fear any shadows.

8

On the sidelines

"Meet Collen; he's our new intern," Maphefo says with a poker face as the young man with a friendly face stretches out his hand to greet me. I know not to expect Maphefo to say "this is Maki, our component manager" so I introduce myself to the young intern. My thoughts run wild. When did we even shortlist and have interviews? I cannot ask Maphefo.

I cast my eyes in Faith's direction as they leave, only to find her also looking my way with a questioning look that was also knowing. I wonder what else we are not privy to. As the two leave, I think briefly about how happy I am that I have been moved out of the office into the open plan, where Faith and I could support each other better.

Faith comes over to tell me she saw the young man the day before when I was out of office attending a meeting. He wasn't introduced the whole day, and it was a bit awkward. Faith later tells me Nana from HR told her that interviews were held four weeks or so ago, and that both Lalang and Maphefo had been on the panel.

No matter how often one gets these surprises, no matter how immune one thinks one has grown immune to these shenanigans, when they hit, it still aches.

I head to Lalang's office for a meeting that was supposed to have happened an hour earlier. She had again set the meeting as early as possible but failed to arrive on time. Like the other meetings where she had been late, or worse, a no-show, there was no courtesy on her part to contact me and let me know. At least this time she had sent an email to say 'we can meet now.' I have to be content with this. It's better than her recent behaviour where she had dumped me in meetings involving other people, without any apology and not a measure of guilt. *I'm being strengthened*, I keep saying to myself. It's a good thing I prepare thoroughly for every meeting. That the chairperson went AWOL did not affect any of the meetings or the work. I continued making excuses for her during meetings. I would never hear the end of it if I acted in the same way, or was simply five minutes late. Do unto others as you would have them do unto you. Or not.

"The email that you sent last night..." I say before Lalang interrupts.

"The information was due yesterday. I know you had sent me something but the framework was missing and I couldn't send anything to Kaitlyn," she says, to my utter dismay.

Lalang is unaware that I know she instructed Maphefo not to give me the information that was supposed to be packaged together with the work I have done. She knows very well I did not have the document, but she sent me an email asking me to send something I did not have and even had the audacity to end her communication with a reminder that the information was due on the day. I had sent all the information I had, and Maphefo being a loose cannon, unintendedly told me the same person who ordered me to send the document had instructed her not to give me the document! Besides, I was out of the office. I can see cases are being built. I take a deep breath.

My eye catches sight of a document on her table as she continues to talk smoke to my frame. The document appears to be a travel plan, complete with names of people. They will be travelling to different places around the country over a period of a month — Lalang, Maphefo, Leonard, Frank, and even the newly joined intern, Collen, together with two other colleagues within the organisation, who are Lalang's friends. There is no 'Maki' or 'Faith' on the list.

She changes the subject as soon as she realises I had been looking at the list. "You know, we're going to be travelling and giving presentations over the next few weeks. But we cannot all go. Some people have to remain and keep the office functional. People like yourself with young kids can stay," she says, making herself appear thoughtful, which is contrary to the usual "people do not want to work" phrase she uses to make us feel bad about wanting to be accommodated when travel plans are devised.

Lalang knows all too well I don't have a problem with work taking me away from home – I just need to be a part of the planning so that, I don't get surprises that would inconvenience me. But she would be damned if she was going to involve me in any planning.

"I overheard Leonard asking her about some travel arrangements. She had to say something after that, I guess. So she comes here and tells me that I have a lot of work I need to do in the office and that was the reason I wasn't going," Faith says laughing as I share with her some weird details of my meeting with Lalang.

"What 'lot of work'?" I ask.

We laugh again. Lalang has reduced Faith's duties to practically printing and binding reports. She calls it 'building a knowledge repository.' Faith is tired of challenging this degrading of her knowledge. We laugh about it a lot, but truly speaking, it is a career-limiting tactic and no laughing matter. We laugh to survive, and when we laugh we laugh from our core. It keeps us joyful despite our troubles, and it keeps us from plotting to avenge or from declaring disputes. It is healing. Painful as this is, revenge is up to karma, not us. There is one thing Faith is clear about though: she would cause a scene if she died and Lalang or Maphefo dared to show up at her funeral.

"I told even my family about this, Maki; I am not joking. Should I be called by my maker while still working here, those two crooked women are not allowed to attend even my memorial service here at work, dare I say. You are to make sure they do not show their devious faces. If I see them at my funeral, I will send sweeping winds to wipe their behinds and throw them to the air, and finally, expose them for the witches that they are."

These utterances are serious but funny. I cannot help but laugh whenever she says this. She says it with an odd blend of laughter and pain.

Apparently, a similar thing once happened with a lady who passed on at the organisation. Work stress, for which her manager was blamed, had put her in hospital for months before she passed away. Her family attended the memorial service with an extraordinary request: her supervisor was not welcome at the service. I don't know what this manager might have done to deserve the humiliation. But if she had been anything like Lalang, she probably deserved it.

"You know, Maki, they hide information from you to make you appear incompetent and to frustrate you until you go down on your knees begging them for organisational intelligence that should be accessible on a shared drive or something," Faith says as I continue to explain what happened.

"And all the while others get spoon-fed. Do you know that while we slave away, all of Maphefo's expected deliverables involve work that has already been completed?" I say as Faith's eyes go right to the back of her head.

"Believe it, Faith, I have seen it. It is work that's been done in the past by other employees. It will be submitted as part of Maphefo's portfolio of evidence. Meanwhile, she would be looking all busy knowing very well her job entails Lalang's travel bookings, the policing she does on her behalf, and her own knitwear patterns that she always prints out."

"That's what she gets performance bonuses for," Faith adds as she packs to leave the office, with the saddest look in her eyes, and I could swear, a cloud of tears as well.

Lalang doesn't give a damn about meaningful work. It's all about pretence for her – so long as something can be produced and submitted, she's happy. I remember how she even tried to let me in on the cheating by telling me how to properly dress and marinade a report to make it all look good at first glance because 'nobody reads the stuff.'

Although her boss pays a lot of attention to typography and overall look and feel, Kaitlyn's intentions aren't to dress the badness out of any report, as they do with supermarket meat by covering its staleness in tantalising sauces. She must have noticed the shock and disappointment in my eyes when she tried to let me in on the shameful secret because she had since tried to act all professional around me.

The downside is that she is now overdoing it, as she often jokes and laughs casually around the likes of Maphefo only to quickly switch to a professional superior demeanour upon my appearance.

I notice something strange on my car as I approach it. Indeed, there are a few new scratches that are visibly man-made, deliberate acts by some evil force who is obviously out to get me. I immediately report to the security office. The cameras at the parking lot had not been working for a week now. I will never know who hated me so much they would scratch my car. It was like my worst fear had come true. Tilly's experience had somewhat cushioned me against the shock and hurt, but still ... how am I to come back here again and park my car here? It's a Friday, and I'm in a hurry to get home. My heart says I should not put something like this past Lalang or Maphefo, but my head cannot comprehend either of them being capable of such evil acts.

What have I done to these people for them to be so hateful towards me? I ask myself as I examine the car for further signs of sabotage. Satisfied that there weren't any more, I jump in my car and drive off while rocking to the sounds of Joyous Celebrations music. This too shall pass, I agree with the lyrics.

9

Gender roles

I have no doubt in my mind about this. None whatsoever. If there is a next life for me, I am not marrying him again unless he comes back as a chef. And by that, I mean one that is as passionate about cooking for me as he is about cooking for his clients. This is my prerequisite, and I am sticking to it.

I suppose I didn't know better back in my early twenties when he swept me off my feet and captured my entire being with just his brilliant mind. I totally adore Makhananisa, but his aversion to prepare a meal is unmatched. Whenever his poor personal 'chef' is not home, dinners are boxed. That sure makes the kids happy but the hopeless romantic in me, married to the hopeless unromantic that is him, can never give up hoping to find a surprise warm meal at home, that one beautiful day.

There is no killing that imagination no matter how many times it has been crushed. It keeps me breathing, and for the most part, also married. It is not fun at all to be married to a so-called realist. But even so, I have to admit they are made for marriage. Go figure.

For the most part, we get each other – me and him. We hold similar views about marriage and life in general. When I think of integrity, I think of him. Together, the two of us can remove all the fluff and lies about relationships and marriage and leave only the real stuff. Or our idea of it. I guess that makes me a realist too. But I refuse to 'get real' about the culture of women automatically assuming kitchen roles. Or bathroom ones for that matter. That's why, no matter how much I love him, I would not marry Makhananisa again if he was not to come back as a chef – or at the very least, a cook.

I have told him this before. I know he said he would marry me again, but that was ten years ago when we'd been married for a number of years. I'm not going to keep asking him this question, because his views might have changed and he would not hesitate to tell me he would marry me with only less meat, if that was his truth. But I know it's not. Even if he had married me for having been bonier, which I was not, being the realist he is, he would already have figured and accepted that with age and babies, one had to add some bits.

Realists make durable husbands. Just not the best lovers. But we women tend to be content having men tell us whatever they know would tickle our fancies – and get them what they want. Unfortunately, we've been made this way - to receive, without too much questioning, the often sugar-coated sweet nothings. We've been programmed to recognise this as love. Even true love.

People like Makhananisa would only make it in long-term relationships if matched with people like me who like to dive and search into the soul. Thank heavens for that. I wouldn't trade my unromantic man for any romantic one out there, though I wouldn't mind if he could change a bit. And he still needs to become a chef, yes.

I catch a group of builders working next door all staring at my husband as he hangs out clothes on the washing line. I don't have to wonder what they must be thinking, saying or what they did not have to say. I bet we would make for a very interesting conversation topic come this evening when weekend makes its plans known to these men at whatever hangout they go to. When will this patriarchy issue ever be laid to rest!? I wonder as I carry the rest of the laundry to the line and join my husband in hanging them. This is exactly how I want to raise my children – this is what I want both my son and daughter to know of the concept of marriage and family. The definition of submission as we have gotten accustomed to, has the potential to kill a modern-day woman if she doesn't put things into perspective for herself. I cannot teach my girl child to succumb to that, and I would be lying to my boy if I taught him that his woman needed no assistance from him in the home front.

Makhananisa and I have taken the day off in preparation for a busy weekend ahead. Tradition decided ages ago that tomorrow, in preparation for the funeral of a distant uncle of my husband whom I've never met, I'm to stay up the whole night cooking as a daughter-in-law. This is one of the things a working mother and wife has to embrace as an indestructible part and parcel of her African being.

The men staring at us are seemingly shocked at my being so comfortable with what in their macho minds I was putting my husband through. I realise in that moment that my unromantic man was probably other women's idea of romantic.

Many would trade the flowers for doing the laundry together. But heck, can't we have all of it, though?! Can't we have a near perfect man who can cook and do laundry with us and still think to have a bunch of plump roses delivered for us at work? Is that too much for a lady to ask?

Men are conveniently comfortable with how we have all been socialised; it suits them. Why do those men stare when a couple is simply working together doing laundry? What is so entertaining about a man hanging the laundry?

Is it because of that myth that a married man doing laundry must have been bewitched by the wife?

"Let them mind their own business and deal with their own household issues," my husband says as I point him to the audience he has attracted. It's a bit unsettling for me because I think I know exactly what they're saying and giggling about. It's always the same: "The poor man must have been given some unmanning concoctions, and that's why he's hanging a woman's clothes in broad daylight."

As though only women were qualified to do laundry. I'm reminded of one old lady, the groom's mother at a wedding, who announced to everyone that her son could wash, iron, clean, cook and bake, and that people should not start saying nasty things about her daughter-in-law when they see her husband onto such household chores.

My husband's no-care comforts me, and I choose to believe that the construction crowd is just spectators. Period. These are the same guys who see nothing wrong with stopping their work, bricks in hand, just to stare at a woman passing on the street. Some of them would even shout what they think to be praises at a woman's beauty, not realising how annoying and intrusive that feels. I cancel them in my mind and, deciding they are no longer there, I continue with my work.

The whole societal unfairness refuses to leave my mind, though. I'm reminded of a time when as a young mother, I would be so exhausted after work that an even more exhausting second shift would have easily destroyed me had my husband not been hands-on.

During this period as a breastfeeding, full-time working mother without a nanny, I once parked my car outside in the street in front of the apartment block we lived in and rushed inside the flat to breastfeed my impatient little one whom I had picked up from the nearby crèche.

I knew that if I started feeding him in the car, he would not let go of the nipple and we would stay in the car forever as he slept on my breast. I would probably have fallen asleep along with him, out on the streets. He always fell asleep on the breast, and I was thinking I could park the car later on or ask my husband to park it for me. As I nourished my baby and watched my favourite soap opera, I too fell asleep and forgot that my car was still outside. The next morning, as I carried my baby to the crèche before I could get in the car and drive to work, I saw a car that looked similar to mine in the same spot. I was shocked when I realised that not only did I forget my car there overnight, but I also didn't even remember this as I laid my eyes on this car that looked like mine. If I could be that tired even with a helpful husband, I shudder to imagine what women who live with dogmatic men must go through. Maybe the cooking issue shouldn't be such a deal-breaker after all.

A friend told me of her cousin who, as a hard-working and exhausted new mommy, once ironed a whole basket full of dirty clothes without even noticing they were dirty. And the stress is not just limited to mothers who work outside the home. Sofia's mother was a stay-at-home mom.

She apparently got so irritated one day when her husband came back home and asked the infamous 'what's for dinner' question, she threw a massive tantrum, and with that, the meat she had on marinade out the window as well. She could not comprehend how her husband failed to understand that she too had been working tirelessly all day, most probably harder than he did.

All she wished for was for someone to cook a meal for her, or at the very least, no one to make any demands on her already used up body. But no one realised just how exhausted she was – not even her hubby. Such is the unacknowledged labour of a new mother.

With laundry done, Makhananisa and I drive to his hometown of Majakaneng. His would be a relaxed evening, even a lovely reunion with family. Mine, on the other hand, was to be a very long, tiresome, sleepless, and unappreciated work night where I would be expected to peel and cook and have not much in the way of rest. I opt for the less desired onions so I could shed my tears at the never-ending labour we've adopted as custom, without attracting any attention.

Also, I much rather choose onion tears than tears caused by smoke from the gas stove, and the other ladies appreciate me for choosing the least desired of all vegetables to chop. I will shed my tears amidst the gossip and sweet small talk that make the practice as fun as it could get.

10

A perfect day at work?

The sky is blue, violets are bluer; I've had enough sleep despite my busy weekend, and no one forgot their pencil cases at home this morning. This is set to be a very beautiful day. Even my son woke up without me having to coax him with reminders of the upcoming long weekend.

My heart melted as he jostled himself into my blankets and wrapped his little hands around me, his sweet smile wiping away any dread for the day as he gathered my melted heart and allowed it to dance with his: "Good morning, Mama. You know, I'm happy, Mama! I may be missing a few of my teeth, but that does not mean I cannot be happy."

What a way to start my day, I thought, smiling at the universe for its little sweeteners. Any morning that my little one wakes up and jumps into my bed is a beautiful one.

I drop the kids off at school and get my usual wave goodbye from the little one and a sharp signal from his sister. I drive off with a contented heart, despite having just dropped off two huge chunks of it.

To add more zest to my morning, even the traffic happens to be smooth sailing. I pinch myself. I hate being a doubting Thomas, but there must be a catch somewhere.

How could one day have so much sweetness in it? But it's still too early to form a verdict. It's only 8am, and I'm just about to enter that unpredictable, devilish place I call my workplace, the one that should, in all honesty, be called a war-place. The idea of war rooms must have been birthed here. I need to compose myself now. I need to wake up from Dreamland as I pull the key from the ignition and with it, the lovely sounds of the uplifting sing-along music that took me to unknown places as it accompanied me to this strange place I typically find myself in for a good one-third of my day, five days a week.

Will I ever like this place? Will I ever again get to work with people that I can relate to, who are not so full of themselves? I hate not knowing what my day will look like. I understand that life is unpredictable and I'm happy dealing with its mood swings but those of people, no!

I take another deep breath, say my short prayers and step out of the car into the unknown that is my typical day at the office. I even manage to greet the security personnel with my usual smile. I would hate to have a repeat of that awful day when they all wondered what had happened to my smile as I walked quietly passed them, without a word – or any awareness of their existence for that matter.

What Lalang had said to me I couldn't possibly have shared, so I didn't answer their inquisitive questions the next day. Still, how could I have allowed myself to be so disturbed as to miss a chance to say hello or goodbye to someone with a smile? I'm terrified of what this place is doing to me. I can't allow work stress to alter my ever-green mood. It scares the life out of me that Lalang was able to get to me that deeply.

That day, just before knockoff time, Lalang called me to her office. "Come closer," she had said, creating a very strong image of myself being pushed out the third floor window, as she asked me to come closer to the window she stood next to.

I walked slowly, wondering if she could be in a good enough mood to want me to delight with her at the sight of lovebirds doing what they do best.

"You see those hawkers out there?"

Her demeanour whispered to me I wasn't going to like this. Of course, I could see the three ladies whose freedom I had often drooled over. They would probably be shocked to hear that someone in this beautiful, air-conditioned building could view theirs as an enviable life.

"One of these days, you will find yourself hustling out there in the streets if you're not careful; you will be like those women selling apples and onions," she said, much to my horror. I managed to let out a swear word before storming out of her office, grabbing my bags and passing through the security section deep in thought.

Granted, those ladies' hustles do not scare me. They seem happier at work than most of us in these beautiful offices. They're always laughing and in a good mood out there.

I cannot say the same for Lalang's moods, though. If Ms Masego is in a bad mood, my day is as good as spoiled. If her partner in crime is not in the office the day has a chance of going well. You see, Ms Masego is like an unconfident teen who thrives on groupies and pleases her friends by doing what they would have her do. If Maphefo is not at work, Lalang is a friendlier person.

What Maphefo has on her is still anybody's guess, though a few birdies mentioned that the loyalty has something to do with a couple of sealed suitcases that exchanged hands at the deathbed of a certain multi-million rand project that Lalang managed.

Maphefo knows all about it, and so she sits like a ticking time bomb that Lalang knows not to rub the wrong way.

I take a long deep breath before the escalator door opens to the weighty air of the third floor. I step out as my son's words of wisdom ring in my head. I paraphrase them to suit my situation and hopefully lift my spirits: *I am happy. I might be sharing a workspace with some scheming vermin, but that does not mean I cannot be happy.* I smile and face the day.

But evil has a way of knowing when a person is happy, content and at peace with oneself. For it is usually at those moments of pure joy that evil likes to strike. This seems to be one of those moments. It seems I can never cushion myself enough from these attacks.

"There is a complaint that came regarding your presentation last week. I'm waiting for that complaint in writing so that we can respond appropriately," Lalang says as she storms into my workstation right after me.

"Oh, okay, Ms Masego; what is the complaint about exactly?" I ask as I put down my handbag and set out to connect the laptop.

"I don't have any details yet. I just know that someone out there phoned the boss's office and delivered a verbal complaint, which they will apparently back up with a formal, written one. I was hoping you could maybe fill me in since you were at that meeting and I was not," Lalang says with surprising enthusiasm and excitement concealed badly behind an awkwardly serious face.

"The meeting went perfectly well as I already reported to you, Ms Masego. There was absolutely nothing from the audience that signalled any measure of discontent, especially something that would have warranted a call to the highest office! Faith can attest to that. But we will just have to wait for that written complaint and deal with its contents when we know what it is about. For now, I won't lose any sleep over it," I say, making sure to put emphasis and attitude into the last part, as I look straight and deeper into her eyes.

"Yes, I mean who complains about a mere typo on a slide?" Lalang says almost without thinking. "We see a lot of serious typos all the time," she continues. I count to ten as I take deep breaths upon realising she actually knows the details about this so-called complaint. She was right about one thing – that we all make mistakes. It should be heart-warming to have heard such a defence, except it came from Lalang. For all I knew, she was the one that set the bees abuzz. And who could forget Lalang's own awkward typo that left the auditorium roaring last year? "Commission for *Pubic* Affairs," I speak the words out, managing a gratified smile as she leaves my workstation.

I share the breaking news with Faith over the phone as soon as Lalang leaves. It did not seem like a good time to rush and share in the bathrooms or to go whisper at Faith's desk. Faith immediately dismisses the so-called complaint as typical Ms Masego-style lies.

"How long will it take for you to learn Ms Masego's ways and her uncanny talent for concocting lies, Maki? Tell me, just how long?" Faith asks me, almost furiously. She was not furious at Ms Masego. She would never put anything past her, especially negativity and lies. She was furious at me for often believing Lalang's tales until they were proven as such.

"You know, Faith, I think I doubt her enough. I some-times cannot get myself to dismiss these stories because I cannot imagine anyone, not even Ms Masego, cooking allegations like this from scratch. That should be tiring, especially for someone her age. She should know that she will forget and get tangled in her own lies sooner or later. Why even bother creating such lies? Something must have been uttered somewhere, and wrong as it already sounds, we shall wait and see."

As we hang up, I see Faith coming up to my desk walking in a seemingly painful manner without the crutches. She's come a long way since the day I met her, which was apparently not long after she'd had an accident that almost left her paralysed. With a fed-up gesture, she picks up my desk phone and instructs me to look up Vera's number. "If there is any complaint that the high office received, she would know."

I listen in awe as Faith's conversation indicates to me that Vera has no clue what complaint Faith was referring to. She signals for me to come closer to the phone so I could listen in. It's clear Vera doesn't know what Faith was on about. I'm still sceptical. Maybe she just cannot divulge inside information. I know Ms Masego is something of a compulsive liar, but this?

Faith gives me an 'I give up on you' look as she leaves my workstation. I know she has worked with Ms Masego all these years, and I was relatively new, but how could anyone make up something like this that could paralyse us, put a brake on the work and destabilise the unit? I choose to believe that there is some smoke somewhere. But it will not have the effect on me that Ms Masego hopes it would have. I am solid and won't be shaken by such things. If she thinks she will destroy my self-esteem this way, she has another thing coming.

I slip into another memory and start thinking that maybe Faith has a point. Ms Masego never fails to surprise in the undesirable creativity department. I recall when I just started working with her and I had to complete some contractual forms. My physical address was required, and I obliged. Hardly ten minutes after leaving her with the two-pager form she was to sign, Ms Masego came to my office and started talking about something that happened during the weekend.

"We had a ladies' club gathering, and we invited a psychologist to present to us. She talked about depression and how a lot of women were unhappy in their marriages." I braced myself for some bragging as I'd already heard that Ms Masego boasts about having the best marriage this side of the Sahara.

"There is this lovely neighbourhood called Malys – beautiful estate – but the psychologist told us that over eighty percent of the wives in those homes were admitted to the Apal hospital for depression, because while they were living in those lovely houses, they were lonely and unable to enjoy anything because their husbands were just never home."

I just couldn't believe what I was hearing because Malys was where I live and I had just handed her the forms with my physical address only a moment ago … and there was no such nonsense anywhere! How could anyone come up with such a tall tale? Is this woman playing with a full deck of cards really?

I am in doubt, but I have to give her the benefit of the doubt. But Faith could be right. If this person could fabricate such incredibly bad lies and even go to the extent of slathering them with over-the-top statistics, surely she could create anything! If I continued to afford her the benefit of the doubt, what sort of lies could she still create?

There was way too much evidence to back Faith's theory, and I would do well to believe it and spare myself some anxiety about this purported complaint because it seems Ms Masego would do just about anything to see me bury my head in shame, if not drop down and die.

Three weeks passed, and still no news of the complaint. I could no longer wait; I had to ask Ms Masego. "I'm still waiting for the written complaint, but you know, I met this woman at a hotel, and she approached me because she saw me with Maphefo. I didn't know her myself, but she works for one of the organisations you presented to. So I asked her about this complaint that we heard about and she said there were some errors in your presentation. I said to her we see errors on presentations all the time but does that warrant calling the head's office to complain? She also said that you said you were new in this unit and at your level that was completely unacceptable. I asked her if it was wrong for someone to say they were new. What's wrong with that? If you are new, you are new."

Who exactly was Lalang fooling with that terrible act of solidarity? It's obvious that it's in her nature to sniff and dig, then put paraffin on the smallest issues she found, only to come to me pretending to have stood up for me. I manage to pretend along.

"Context is everything, Ms Masego, more so in this case. I would probably understand if they were claiming that I'd told them I was new in the context of not knowing an answer to some question. But where I remember saying I was new was at the beginning during introductions; I said this because the lady who was welcoming us knew Faith very well but didn't know my name and I had to somehow respond to that. I also said I was not yet here when they started referring to meetings that predated my joining this unit. Not once did I respond to a question by saying I was new! These people have serious issues and they must just send that formal complaint already. I'm sick of this!"

I exit her office and call Faith to the pause area to share this conversation. For the first time, I also share with her the *depressed wives in my neighbourhood* tale. Faith bursts out laughing uncontrollably, prompting me to scan the horizon to see if there was anyone around who could be disturbed by the loud laugh. This woman can laugh until the cows come home. And the more Ms Masego ill-treated her, the louder her laughs became. At least, so it seemed.

"They need to know that their behaviour is not punching any holes here," she says beating her chest.

"About this depression thing, this woman likes this condition so much. Remember I told you she asked me if I was depressed when she wanted to know why I was taking two days off? Did I tell you how excited she was to share the news of our former colleague, Theko's hospital admission due to depression two years ago? I mean she even circulated details of the poor guy's illness to every-one, when she fails to share work-related information with us. It would tickle her so much if one of us could get depressed. Oh my goodness, I can only imagine how chuffed she would be. The entire building would know; even the doves and lizards would be kept abreast."

It's my turn to laugh now, having completely forgotten my earlier worry about making noise. The woman's obses-sion with depression, especially as may be related to Faith and myself, is just incredible. Who knows, perhaps she has already told the doves we're showing signs of depres-sion. Maybe we should laugh louder without checking ourselves so that she realises that if any of us was at all depressed, she was the trigger. We are happy so long as she was not in our midst. I would even dare say we are much happier people than she could ever be, even with her self-proclaimed marriage among marriages.

I thank Faith for the therapy, and we return to work, feeling light as air. Ms Masego must just give up trying to destroy me, or us for that matter. We are way too strong for her fragile little ego, way too smart and resilient. She will destroy herself in the process of trying to destroy us. She is up against very strong characters and the sooner she realised she was striking some rocks, the better for her. She will fall into all these holes she is forever digging for us, and when that happens, she won't be able to pick herself up.

I will get back to work. I will continue to do the best I can. I will not let my light get feeble under Ms Masego's dark shadows. I will continue to shine my light no matter whose eyes are getting damaged by it. I will do my best no matter how many compliments are withheld. And no matter how creative the lies get, I will keep recognising them and laughing them off, as loud as I could.

At home, I work well into midnight on a report that had to be submitted in a few days. Just as I was starting to enjoy my early morning sleep, Motheo comes into the room.

"I have a sore tummy and the air keeps getting stuck in my throat when I burp."

"Oh, this is not good," I say as I drowsily feel his tummy and find it hot as a coal stove.

Lalang was just talking about absenteeism in our meeting yesterday and here I find myself, with a report due and a sick child whom I cannot expect to be fine by morning. I think, as though by some law of attraction, Lalang attracts the same things she focuses on.

They say one will keep having the same experiences up until they have absorbed the lesson nature is trying to teach them. And in Lalang's case, she seriously needs to start trusting us. We're not some irresponsible kids who would just opt to stay home and not come to work for some dodgy reason. Whatever you're aiming to teach, Lord, please leave my child out of it. Please, use other means to teach and remind her of what being a mother to small kids is all about.

As though the universe was shaking its head on my request, my phone dies. And it does so just after Makhananisa leaves the house. I search for the old phones and insert my card in one. But none of my colleagues' numbers are on the sim card. I start wondering if it was me who had some lesson to learn. *Relax, Maki. Yes, relax. The world will go on, and surely you can send an email and inform Lalang as you send her the report.* Indeed, I have worked my eyelids off on this one. I will take a breather and focus on my baby. To hell with Lalang's mistrust and accusations. I know my truth and will stand for it.

By a stroke of luck, Frank sends me a message to inform me that he was not feeling well himself. I immediately ask him for Lalang's numbers and send her a message. I expect no response from her, and sure enough, I get none. Though I've cushioned myself against such coldness, I'm still surprised when it actually happens.

Surely Lalang has kids, and she knows how we mothers feel when our little ones have even a minor ailment! She should, therefore, know that no attack in this world would be frightening enough if my child's health is at risk, and she should know I don't give a thing about her threats. Maybe when my kids get older, I too will forget and will fall short of giving young mothers the necessary support. But I doubt I would ever treat people this way. When it comes to their kids, even the most cowardly of mothers would dare to show someone like Lalang one of her fingers.

I get myself and the boy ready, and we head for the paediatrician's rooms. By the time we get there, Motheo is struggling to walk, and I'm petrified. He asks me to carry him because his legs are painful. What in the world is going on? I carry him for the short distance to the room, and we sit. I don't want to draw too much attention, so I pretend my carrying him had nothing to do with his inability to walk. I say my prayers and feel assured he will be fine. I don't want to alarm his dad; I would rather wait to hear from the doctor before contacting anyone. By the time we are called in to see the doctor, the boy's legs have all but given up. Now it is clear he couldn't walk.

"His reflexes are fine, so we know it is not nerve damage, thankfully," says Dr Mano to my slight relief.

"What then, could be the problem, Doctor?" I ask anxiously.

"We will run some tests. In the meantime, we will give him some antibiotics. Would you like us to observe him in hospital or would you rather observe him at home while we wait for the results?"

My mind goes into overdrive. I think of all the wrong diagnoses that occur in hospitals and especially wrongful amputations. I shed a tear as I imagine the worst. I ask the doctor for a moment as I check with my husband.

"I'm coming right away," he says after having pleaded with me not to have our son admitted.

"Don't rush, please drive safely," I plead with him in return.

"Take him for these blood tests, and make sure he starts on his antibiotics today. If his condition hasn't improved at all by tomorrow, please bring him right back. If he shows some improvement, bring him back in two days," the doctor instructs me, handing me the prescription.

I'm glad we were given the option of nursing him at home. We head to the laboratory for the tests, boy on my back. Just as we prepare to go out, Makhananisa enters, and with him an overwhelming sense of calm and a knowing that all will be okay. He gets the medication from the pharmacy and takes Motheo home in his car. I follow. We give him a dose of the antibiotics and the other prescribed meds.

"You know, Dr Mano was actually shocked at the dosage that the doctor at the emergency section had given the other day; she says it is a dose fit for newborn babies. Definitely wrong and inadequate for a child of Motheo's age and weight."

Makhananisa shakes his head. We both have a strong suspicion that the miniature dosage given the previous weekend has something to do with the state our boy is in. We say our prayers and go to sleep, in faith.

Nothing could have prepared me for the sadness I feel in the morning when Motheo doesn't come jumping on my bed as usual. Much as I do not like that habit on many days when all I want is to sleep, not having him there and knowing the reason why he was not there, throws me into a deep sadness. Regretting why I let him sleep alone, I walk to his room, hoping he isn't awake and just sitting there waiting for one of us to take him to the bathroom. Thankfully he is still sleeping, and it's my presence that wakes him up. He attempts to get out of bed but says he was feeling some pain. His dad enters and helps him to the bathroom. I reach for my phone and send a message to Lalang to tell her I still would not be able to come to the office. Silence, as always, is her response.

"She says you must call her," reads a message from Faith an hour or so after I send one out to both of them. I hesitantly dial Lalang's number.

"I have no problem if your child is sick, but I should not hear it from third parties," she says. "I sent you a message yesterday and today," I respond. She claims not to have received any of those messages. That I'm in distress doesn't cross her controlling mind, and she hangs up without so much as a well wish for my son. As far as I am concerned, she can go take an icy cold shower if she wants; I'm not going to work until my boy is absolutely fine.

Makhananisa reluctantly leaves for work after I encourage him to go. The patient is in good spirits; seemingly oblivious of what is at stake. Maybe he knows something we don't know. I give him cereal, then his medication. I then get some hot water and start to rub his legs. He sleeps as I carry on rubbing and praying.

By midday, he can stand without complaining of pain. I know he is getting better and we do not need to rush back to the doctor. By the afternoon he can walk with support, and by evening he is limping by himself. Thank God! The results the next day indicate some autoimmune reaction which could be attributed to having received an unsuitable dose of antibiotics. I feel sad that the dose was more than just ineffective – it was also hazardous. The doctor is relieved, and so are we. Lalang can wait. Life is not all about her and her ego. Some of us are busy raising children, whether she acknowledges it or not. If this was her idea of absenteeism, so be it. I was not going to give her the presenteeism she was demanding. Motheo is running around by the end of the day; I should be able to go to work tomorrow.

When I'd just started working, I used to love Thursdays for the promise of Friday. But with years of slavery, bad working experiences, ridiculous bosses, and age, I appreciate promises less because when it is Thursday, I promise you Friday never seems to arrive. I've told myself to forget promises and love Friday and not the smell of it. Even Motheo himself, at six years of age, appreciates Fridays. He even has a favourite pair of Friday underwear.

"It's a bit cold, aren't you wearing your jersey? I ask as we prepare to leave the house.

"Mom, I never feel cold on a Friday," he responds, leaving me dumbfounded. I am taken aback. But I am glad he is feeling well enough to go to school, and that I too could wrap up the week at the office.

There's a meeting waiting, carefully planned for when I return to the office. As expected, Lalang talks about absenteeism and how people don't want to work. "If anyone does not want to be here, they must apply for an internal transfer to another unit; I mean I will support that," she says. Then on and on she goes about how some people are hard-working and leave their families at the last minute if called to do so. "We all have husbands. Some of our kids may be older, but we are married, we have husbands, you know.

"Sometimes I worry about who will lead this unit when I go on retirement. I am concerned." Personally, I don't think for a second that Lalang's worries have anything to do with leadership, productivity or progress; nor does it have to do with Joe public out there. I think she is just spewing as much poison as she could, like a serpent in its final moments as it tries to defy its inevitable end.

"Oh, you think we are eyeing that position you hold, Madam? We are not. We are not cemented to this place. The world is vast, and we could get the same or better opportunities out there. Who would want a position that is bound to grow horns as soon as one occupies it? There is no succession plan in place and save for Maphefo, you have done nothing in the way of preparing any one of us to ever take over the baton. You have failed to involve me in the important nitty-gritties, and you're making sure that you hide from me as much as possible. If this is what that position would turn me into, I would rather be where I'm now, thank you very much."

I respond because Lalang's words are a direct accusation as I'm the one that might be applying for that position. She has hidden as much as possible from me and will retire without sharing her knowledge when the system finally kicks her in the rear and forces her out into retirement. The closer that time gets, the more in denial she becomes about the inevitable. The older she grows, the shorter her skirts become. Faith and I have recently had to defend her against the mocks of two colleagues from another unit who asked us why her skirt was missing because she was wearing what seemed to be just a top and not even stockings underneath. We've had to tell them that "one is as young as one feels" and that even Lalang is at liberty to dress however she desires. We had to defend her because if we joined the critics, we would eventually be asked why we weren't telling her how odd her outfit looked, and we knew that talking to her was not an option.

A couple of us were sadly very aware of other symptoms of denial and perhaps even cognitive decline. A month after her normal retirement age had passed, Lalang was busy telling everyone how tired she was of the politics in the organisation. I recall how, when she complained to us in a meeting, I asked myself why she was not just retiring because age was on her side. I even expected those complaints to be followed by news that she was soon to retire, and not just the usual 'I'm leaving in two years' story she had consistently been telling, apparently for the past three. But to my shock, she instead announced that she was leaving at the end of the next month – not on another holiday, but to join another organisation.

I think at that point everyone knew that being hired at retirement age by that particular organisation was quite unheard of. But still we all waited for the official announcement. It never came. Just as Faith had predicted. The date came and passed, and she continued to complain about Kaitlyn and everyone and everything else, as we continued to wonder why somebody who is so entitled to retirement was complaining to us instead of simply packing up. The only thing that made her shoes too difficult for anyone else to fill was that the laces were constantly tied in a certain impractical, tangled manner only she was privy to.

I liken Lalang's retirement phobia to that of a gentleman I had worked with. I recently bumped into him at a shopping mall, and I was puzzled when his initial question to me: "Maki, do you know what happened to me?" was followed by a very simple and natural "the system kicked me out; I retired."

Faith insists Lalang cannot bear to think of leaving us here to enjoy the fresh air in her absence, that is why she will wait to be kicked out by the system. "I'm telling you, Maki, Bonang from Human Resources did the same thing. She was even going around bragging and saying 'I was going to retire at my normal retirement age, but because of this one and that one, I'm going to stay. They will stay wide-eyed waiting for my retirement letter, but it will not come.'"

"I find this so hard to believe, Faith. Are you telling me it is possible for a grown person, an elderly one even, to be so childish? Did blatant spitefulness override such important decisions in her life?"

"She did not make it much of a secret, Maki. She told all who cared to listen that other people would be overjoyed to see her go and this is precisely why she wouldn't go. But five years go by very quickly and where is she today? Those people are still there, and her late retirement was timed out eventually. You wait and see just how quickly it goes for this family member too."

"But you yourself said you will take early retirement, and my calculation tells me you will reach that before Lalang reaches that age when she will be kicked out by the system."

"I know. What else I know is that I am not leaving until Lalang does. I will not give her that satisfaction, Maki. She is older than me so let her retire first."

"Now you are like Bonang and Lalang!" We burst out in laughter.

"You do not know, Maki. That Lalang tormented me so much that I want to be here to see her go. I want her to get itchy sitting at home with the unsavoury awareness she is no longer in charge, and there is not a damn thing she can do about it! After she retires, I will give myself a year or so to finally have a pleasant work environment –

one that would be well set for results," Faith says as tears immediately build up in her eyes.

"Do you know she is the one person in this entire unit who takes leave when her husband has a cold, yet she sees foul when innocent young children, who cannot take care of themselves, are being taken care of by their mothers, who just so happen to be her subordinates at work?"

"You know, Faith, whenever she talks about having a husband too in response to our caring for our young, I wish I could ask her if she bathes and feeds him. Who knows, maybe it's the secret for her milk and honey marriage."

"Maybe we should give her the forms or throw her a retirement party like Sizwe suggested," I say, amusing myself in the process.

What Faith wanted more than anything was to see some of her ideas, which had been lying dormant for years, implemented for the betterment of the unit and of our customers.

It was sad that Lalang consistently shot down her ideas while playing angel's advocate to all of Maphefo's, many of which became frail and died natural deaths before any results could be seen.

A lot of resources have also been wasted, because as far as funds were concerned, Lalang was happy to spend on anything as long as it would, in the eyes of the powers that be, conjure up images of a team hard at work. Spend she had to. Even if it meant using the organisation's funds to support Maphefo's ill-fated ideas, such as purchasing useless items like the branded files that were stacked up in the storeroom. I wonder if they're still there because she had jested that she wanted them to be taken to the dumps, lest they got discovered one day.

The problem is that, when it comes to mismanagement and misappropriation of funds, everyone is blinded to their own contribution, no matter how subtle. Everyone sees the stick in another's eye. And Lalang is no different. It's an open secret she had raised a lifestyle audit concerning me, with the ethics unit.

The ethics unit manager, David, did not exactly shout it from the rooftops, but his words sounded like a clear warning that my manager was suspicious of my lifestyle, or to be more precise, her perception of it. "I'll tell you one thing Maki, those higher in rank don't want to see their subordinates being able to afford the same things they can afford. If you want them to leave you in peace, continue driving your rundown car that smokes like a chimney, drips oil and produces noise irritating enough to wake the dead. Should they bump into you at the same pricey stores they go to, or worse, should they notice that you drive a car that is almost as shiny as theirs, you will be in for a high jump as they push you down to a level they've made up for people in your salary range. If you want them happy, pretend you are struggling and wear cheap clothes often."

I could tell from his words that I had been scrutinised because my "lifestyle seemed rather comfortable for someone at my salary level."

After interviewing me, David proceeded to tell me that managers sometimes just look at someone's lifestyle and make conclusions because they themselves are bad at managing money and are therefore not enjoying their high salaries. "But those that are good at managing their finances are judged by those that do not understand," he reiterated. I just knew.

But I truly don't get it. I've been working and earning for well over fifteen years, and by now, obviously, a couple of million bucks would have gone through my bank account in the way of salaries only. Why should I not have captured and saved at least one of those millions? Why shouldn't I be able to afford to live where I live if I have any financial sense at all? Why wouldn't anyone afford to buy something they wanted if they've been earning for years? What do those senior to us think we do with our earnings – feed it to the doves?

By the end of my meeting with David, I was certain about two things. The first certainty is that David was talking to me after having scrutinised my finances and found nothing untoward.

Secondly, Lalang's warning to me about joining the street vendors wasn't just an empty threat driven by the unpleasant emails we had exchanged on the day, following her amendment of my performance assessment to say I had 'assisted' in a funding proposal that I had in fact developed; she was convinced she'd gotten me!

But sometimes I so want to channel the energy and fighting spirit of some of the women I observed back at the village while growing up. They were not common, low-class street fighters like the seemingly sophisticated Ms Masego actually is. They were valiant. And no matter how bravely I confront the situation with Ms Masego, I never seem to be able to do it the way they would have done it.

If I were anything like them, I wouldn't confront Ms Masego in private. No, I would stand centre stage and hurl all manner of profanities her way. I would elegantly shove my skirts in my underwear and dare her twofaced behind to a good fight that would settle it once and for all. I would tell her that I am no cheese-girl to mess with, that I grew up in a village fighting boys for water and breathing space and would never be defeated by any common girl like her. I am way tougher than she could ever imagine.

And after I am done with her, I wouldn't unhitch my skirts, no, I would take the fight right to my neighbours who dared put bricks atop my boundary wall without so much as asking for my permission. I would sort all of them out, once and for all. I am sick and tired of their uncontained stupidity creeping into and affecting my life.

One day I am going to succeed at channelling Sera's energies. And when that day comes, all these bullies would be left without tongues to lick their wounds. But until I finally succeed at channelling those blunt and gutsy women, I will keep making lemonades from all the lemons thrown at me. What I shall not do is drop down and die from my meekness.

But there are times when I get home and look at my kids and wonder how they would feel if they knew how their mommy – their queen – was being treated at work. Do the likes of Ms Masego ever think as deeply about people? That they are more than just this creature under them in terms of organograms? That there are people out there that hold this very person in high esteem, and would probably have to be jailed if they found out how somebody was ill-treating them? I shed a tear. A grown-up like me being blatantly lied to, talked down at and often reprimanded like a child? What would my kids think? How would they feel?

I've thought so often about this and never for a moment did I think I would see the day when Lalang would use this same argument to describe how wrong it was for her own manager, Kaitlyn, to demean grownups like her. "You know – one is a venerated wife and mother at home, but one comes to work to be undermined, disrespected and be referred to as a dumb dongle by a colleague. Imagine! You come here, and you're told how incompetent and stupid you are and made to feel like you are nothing! Sometimes I just feel like leaving this place."

I was flabbergasted as Lalang used the same analogy I always reflect on. What strikes me is how as human beings we often only recognise wrong when we're at the receiving end. Even as we name it, we still fail to relate it to our own sins and see ourselves as the perpetrator. We can lament until the cows come home about what someone else does to us, and still not see any similarities to what we ourselves inflict on others. And our natural inclination is to listen to the person instead of pointing out that they did this exact thing to us, or saying 'the way you feel about Kaitlyn is precisely how you make me feel.'

As for Lalang leaving the organisation, the only thing I can think of is a silent prayer in my heart, for God to please, please make the days shorter so that this elusive departure day would arrive while some of us were still holding tightly to the sanity pole that was rapidly being taken down by quicksand.

11

Bedroom shadows

I do not want this woman in my bedroom. Not even on a hot day would her cold shadow be welcome anywhere near my private space. But she has once again found her way in. How does she do this?

I try my level best to leave her and all of hers as soon as I get out of the office building, but she tries her silly best to follow me even to this sacred place that is my private love nest. No matter how carefully I inspect the walls, I cannot find any cracks that she could possibly use to invade my intimate space and attempt to control it the way she does my workspace.

Why am I letting her in, though? This is the one place where I'm entitled to be free from her, her friends, and their wayward ways. But here I am, regurgitating and deliberating over the day's most unpalatable occurrences.

How could one person do so much damage to people's lives, their peace of mind and sanity? And how could she do so with a straight face, pretending to be as harmless as a lamb? Even I get fooled by her every now and then, and I find myself looking at and listening to her and wondering if there was a slight chance I was wrong about her and that she was nothing but good inside.

If she could still fool me after so many incidents and so much evidence of how sneaky and malicious she is, what more about those that only get to experience her smooth voice? True, Lalang epitomises a wolf in sheep's clothing, and with an innocent voice tone, too.

I can never get used to her destructiveness. How could she have lied about me like this? Failing to invite me to meetings like she usually does, and then rubbing salt to the already open wound by telling people that I was expected at the meeting and she had no idea why I was absent! I already knew she had lied as usual, but I still had to dig through my emails and appointments, just to be sure of this. Because how does one ever get used to such malice? I never received an invitation and I'm hearing that she told everyone that I was invited and she has no idea why I was a no-show.

I try by all means to let her out, but my head cannot stop talking to me about her. I figure though that since I allowed her in, I would need to somehow show her the door, even if I had to kick her to the curb. I look at the peacefully sleeping Makhananisa next to me. What would he think of me if he knew I let Lalang inside our bedroom? He knows just how difficult the woman makes my life at work. I head for the loo in the hope that it might just help me sleep if I made the trip.

My longtime fear of the dark is overshadowed by the unsavoury thoughts that occupy my mind. I return from the loo, and instead of gently getting back under the covers, taking care not to wake my husband, I jump in as my overimaginative brain reminds me just how gruesome it would be if tonight happened to be that night I have dreaded my entire existence.

It could be tonight's overwhelming darkness that makes me finally bump into that someone that did not necessarily exist. How would I react? I manage to do exactly the opposite of what I intended when I avoided the light switch and chose to step into the darkness: I wake up my husband by literally jumping into bed in fear of bumping into the figure. I swear it's bound to happen one day. If I don't bump into this non-existent figure, one of his family members may one day just push or slap me. I would look with all the intensity my eyes could manage; I would shut my eyes tight then blink in the hope that I would see clearer. But I would know for certain that what I just came in contact with cannot be seen with the naked eye. Who would I slap back, push back or say 'excuse me' to? Would I even think to avenge or apologise or would I just die in cold fear?

Luckily Makhananisa falls right back to sleep as I try to explain that I fell, not from the ceiling, but from the dark corners of my imagination. For a moment I wish that Lalang was more imagined than real. I know she wouldn't hesitate to use my fear of the dark as a weapon to say that my experiences at work were nothing but the result of my overactive imagination too.

I say my prayers and ask God to bind the devil and all that belongs to him which might be lurking anywhere around my home and my life. That all evil may be sent straight to its home where it belongs. That any enemies may be confused and their plans derailed, that they may fall into the very traps that they've laid for me.

I pause mid-prayer and question my choice of words. Was it in keeping with God's word and nature to ask of Him to make anyone fall into some trap, even if they were the ones that would have laid the trap for another? I recall that it comes from the Word itself. I wrap up my prayer and start to feel a little easier as I immediately recall the comforting conversation with Raphesu, one of the people who have had the ill-fated opportunity of working with and reporting to none other than Ms Lalang Masego in the past.

"I assure you, Maki, Lalang is the best example of how not to manage or lead," Raphesu had said with an emphasis on the 'not.' "What sort of senior manager would attempt to embarrass other senior managers reporting to her, in front of junior managers and staff? But I tell you, this is her speciality. She thrives on that kind of thing. For your peace of mind and sanity, please don't take any of it personally, we have all been there. She doesn't put the well-being of employees or the organisation at the top of her priorities. All she knows is to gossip, connive and destroy; divide and conquer is her management style. And if your leadership style clashes with hers, as I would imagine it does, you will be at odds, and nothing significant will be achieved. And that framework she is trying to blame on you has been around for more than eight years now, long before you were appointed to your position. And I'm sorry to say, but that project will never go anywhere under her leadership."

His encouraging words echo through my mind, a fraction louder than the annoying voices that revisited my head earlier.

The framework was indeed drafted ages before I started working with Lalang. When I started, I had to give input on it. I wished I could start it afresh because it seemed no matter how much I tried to get it fixed, it was built on a foundation that was rocky and shaky. Can you imagine my anger and absolute disbelief when suddenly its poor quality was blamed on me? It felt like a trap, and that's exactly like Lalang.

Other than the framework issue, I struggle to come to terms with the fact that she continues to take people like Maphefo with her to all the meetings without saying a word to me or to Faith. I am starting to understand better now what Faith must have gone through prior to my arrival. Though she had repeatedly told me how it felt and I empathised with her, finding myself in the same position sure took my comprehension of her pain to epic levels. I now understand better what she meant when she said "I was new and instead of bringing me on board, Lalang would take Maphefo everywhere with her, give her all the opportunities and exposure available, and then turn around and tell me that Maphefo was cleverer than me and for that matter, much more cleverer than all the other middle managers in the organisation.

How am I to get to Lalang's twisted level of clever then if I am not afforded even a fraction of the exposure that Maphefo enjoys? She is the reason Maphefo is so full of herself. If she is any cleverer why has she stayed in the same position for close to a decade? The sad thing is that she takes Maphefo and puts her on this jelly-made pedestal, and then she turns around and diminishes her when she's not looking. She would never promote her. Deep down, she likes nobody other than herself. She only serves her own interests."

Faith is right. During the first few days in the unit, Lalang told me that Maphefo overrates herself and that she was not as good as she thought she was. So I know exactly what Faith is talking about. Lalang is a classic example of a rat that stings you and then blows air on your wound pretending to be healing you while in fact, it is putting you to sleep so that it could continue to do with you as it pleases.

If only Maphefo could know what Lalang actually thinks of her! But Faith insists that even Maphefo herself is just trying to cope by scratching Lalang's back. She insists that she knows Lalang is destructive and has, in the past, told people that Lalang single-handedly destroyed the unit. This utterance according to Faith did land on Lalang's ears. "Who is fooling who? They are all crooked! They are all pretending."

Regardless of all the evidence that the madness has everything to do with Lalang's inherent makeup, and little, if anything at all, to do with me, I still find myself hurting as I watch a snake basically going about the normal business of, well, being a snake. What I battle to completely digest is how anyone could be so cunning. Be that as it may, I could never resort to scratching Lalang's back, filling my nails with all manner of dirt. She could go jump if she thinks that I am going to obey at all cost in the quest to get her to remove the imperfect lenses with which she chooses to see me.

I turn towards the side table, and the clock screams at me to cleanse my thoughts and get to sleep already. I didn't realise how much time had passed since I lay awake, going over the events of one of my less than perfect days at work.

I manage to convince myself that it's my ego that makes the whole situation painful even as I know it has so much to do with Lalang's character and management style. Still, I think maybe my ego causes me to care way too much about what others think of me.

I doze off as soon as a familiar calm hits me: *I know myself. I know what I am capable of achieving in a healthy work environment. I have nothing to prove to anyone and anyone that chooses to believe Lalang and Maphefo's big mouths, can knock themselves out.*

I don't recall what my dream was about, but judging by how rested I feel in the morning, I know I was in a peaceful dreamland. I wake up and face another uncertain day at work.

12

The things we ate during famine season

I am at pains to withhold my sympathy, looking at her and trying hard to not show any emotion as Lalang explains how unwell she is feeling. *No. No well wishes for this woman, no!*

My inner voice keeps reminding me that she deserves no such sympathy from me. I am tired of being nurturing to someone who has never been nurturing to me. And today, contrary to all the religious and cultural teachings I have consumed about not doing it, I finally do unto her as she always did to me. I want to give her a taste of her own bitter medicine and to do that I have to stoop to her cold level. I know that people like Lalang who dish out bitterness without guilt, usually cannot stand the same treatment when it is dished out to them. They take it hard and would be sure to tell others what a terrible person you are.

But it had to be done.

I listen to my inner voice. You see I had had good practice earlier while I was driving to work. A biker sped past a convoy of cars, revving annoyingly at intervals as he passed some of the cars, including mine. He revved so hard and the noise pierced through my closed window right into my already aching right ear. But moments later I was saying to myself *I so wish karma was always this swift.* My sinful wishes for him were too soon realised, and the other motorists and I were forced to watch as his bike veered off the road, spinning before it came to rest beneath a tree.

He was lucky not to have been thrown off. I've heard horrific stories of searches for certain body parts after bike accidents. Though I had screamed in horror, I managed, like the other motorists, to drive on as though nothing had happened. But even in our annoyance, I'm certain we would have stopped had we not seen him getting up and dusting himself. Such is human nature.

So it's not too difficult now to turn a deaf ear to Lalang's sick cries. I still hate what I'm allowing her behaviour to turn me into, but some things, I feel, need to be done.

My cold thoughts are interrupted by the noisy ring of my mobile phone.

"Is that Mmarena's mother?" the woman on the other side asks politely, yet firmly.

"Yes, it is," I respond nervously.

Oh my God, what could possibly have happened to my daughter?

What possibly could have happened at school?

Is she ill; was she in a fight?

I knew it would happen one of these days – she had fainted just like I had also fainted at school when I was her age. It had to happen today because I too had been less than cordial to at least two people today, which I thought was justified. Karma doesn't care who started the fight, it seems. I was still guilty of revenge and being unforgiving. Now look, something has happened to my innocent child because of my sins.

But the caller's voice doesn't sound in the least disconcerting.

I never knew I could have so many questions in my mind in a matter of seconds. This is how it must be like when a person was about to die, and they say "your whole life flashes in front of you." My mind clogs and I feel faint as I waited for the caller to explain the reason for her call. It felt like forever.

"Everything is okay, Ma'am. It's just that your daughter arrived late for school for the second time this week."

My wild and windy thoughts and visions of my daughter lying helplessly on some cold floor are suddenly suspended at the buzzing of her comforting words. She clearly knows how parents feel about calls such as this one.

"Please accept my sincere apologies, Ma'am. I dropped her off this morning, and I'm aware that she was late. The traffic was unbearable."

"Oh, I'm glad you're aware of this, Mrs Mako. As much as late coming disturbs us, we get some sort of relief when we hear that at least the parent knows the cause, because I tell you, these kids can get up to no good."

"I know, Ma'am, I know. And as parents we can only be grateful to the school for having such strict measures in place; an early warning is the key as far as kids' behaviour and safety are concerned."

We say our goodbyes. And mine is followed by a sigh of relief that nothing was wrong with my child. The life of a parent can be too hectic at times.

My critical thoughts flush in. This thing called 'spectator value' is such a strange phenomenon. Why do we humans like staring at accident scenes so much? I also wish more people, especially youngsters who have just joined the labour force, could live closer to work, especially when they are renting.

I stayed within a good walking distance from work for more than five years and what a delight it was! They just have no idea what they're missing out on. Living closer to work would save them a lot in money and headaches. Traffic is certainly a problem and we can all do our bit to alleviate it. But young people these days shun the good old suburbs adjacent to the cities where they work, and prefer to stay in more affluent suburbs far from their workplaces.

When I share my sentiments with Faith she tells me that unlike us when we started out, young workers these days are able to acquire a car as soon as they start working – that's if they did not start off with some wheels from the family already. "I certainly remember those years when we walked three kilometres or so to work," I say in agreement with Faith.

"Surely those managers must have had an idea what hurdles we crossed just to be at work every morning. But they would look intimidatingly at their wristwatches whenever they would see any of us coming in five minutes late. What they never bothered to understand was how hectic our mornings were. As they cruised in their luxury, air-conditioned vehicles all they could think of was beating us juniors to the office door. Shame on them!"

"That's absolutely true, Maki," Faith adds. "While they would still be in their dream state many of us would already have kicked off our blankets. When they would still manage to crawl back into bed after answering an intrusive bathroom call, some of us would have already been up preparing breakfast and lunchboxes for the family. We then would have had to bath and prepare our young ones for school and crèche before the managers' alarm clocks sounded."

"Shame on them for conveniently forgetting what life was like for those of us at the bottom of the ladder. As they drove to the office, my friend and I would leave our flats on foot, challenging heavy rains, and applying our well-practiced ducking skills on the way as a few obnoxious motorists occasionally swerved, seemingly on purpose, to hit the puddles near the sidewalks so that the water would splash us pedestrians. We noticed how, most often, black motorists either completely avoided hitting those pools of water or would pass slowly and gently whenever there was water that could splash on us and spoil our work suits. Those were the drivers that seemed to understand how arriving at the office with a ruined outfit had the potential to spoil way more than a black girl's day."

I take a deep breath as I leave Faith's company to digest the events of the day out on the one balcony not much the fancy of smokers.

13

More than channelling

I resolve to ignore Ms Masego's crabby stare as I pass by her office, greeting her with a smile. I notice as she looks at her watch in that intimidating manner. She's not going to say anything, I think.

She has slowed down a bit since that day when Sizwe had mustered enough courage to respond to her "work starts at 7:30" statement with his own question: "Oh, am I late? Did the bread burn in the oven?"

Lalang is pretty old school. She fails to recognise that people like Sizwe work so hard, probably harder than most early comers who have social meetings around the pause areas, stand aimlessly at the water coolers or spend time doing Lord knows what on their computers before everyone else arrive.

People like myself, Faith and Sizwe would never put lunch or teatime ahead of work. We simply would not take lunch if we had urgent work to complete. Lalang should get over herself because nobody, not even her controlling self, has control over such unpredictable factors as traffic.

I pass to see some light at the end of the tunnel – the people who help make it bearable to come to work every morning. Colleagues who endure whatever negativity and still manage to focus on their work.

"I am blessed, my sister; how are you?" responds Thabiso in his characteristic holy tone. I wrap up the greeting with similar affirmations and move to greet Lindi.

"Good morning, good morning, how are you?" Lindi chants in all her bubbly glory. How I will miss these two interns when their term ends in a couple of months! We know their contracts, unlike those of other interns in other units, will more likely not be extended, if history was to be relied on. With previous interns – even those she used as spies and promised heaven and earth to –Lalang's modus operandi was always to turn cold on them towards the end of their contracts. Everyone felt sorry for those that fancied themselves Lalang's favourites because we knew she held none's interests at heart.

Maphefo stares at me with lifeless eyes as I pass. I had initially heavily criticised Faith when she told me she had stopped greeting Maphefo. I would never have imagined I would see the day when I too would get sick of simply saying hello to a colleague.

Most of us had stopped wasting our energy on greeting her because she never bothered to greet any of us who were not Ms Masego's favourites. Not even Thabiso's firm sanctity could hold. My sister, Modiegi, always says that pompousness is a freebie, so if someone acts all snobbish on you, take advantage of the fact that it is always freely available, and return the favour. Thank goodness we can all have access to a bit of vanity when we need it.

In the past, passing without greeting would feel almost as if I was pricking myself with needles, but I'm long past feeling guilty now. One cannot completely blame Maphefo, though; she practically controlled the unit and was always a step ahead of everyone on matters of the unit. She could be forgiven for acting as though she was the best thing since sliced bread. She gets away with silly mistakes as far as work is concerned, and she successfully acts like the perfect angel in front of Ms Masego, while she could never be found at her workstation when Lalang was not in the office. Lalang's absence presents her with a chance to paint the town red and come back to the office only to knock off and call it a day. Because she would be the one knowing in advance about Lalang's absence, some colleagues even started observing her behaviour as an alarm bell to announce Lalang's absence for the day. Pity that Ms Masego was set on listening to, and believing Maphefo's lies about what others do in her absence. More unfortunate is that Ms Masego's character and style of management require of her to always keep little spies around her. The relationships often descend quickly to co-dependency as the personalities feed on each other's insecurities and grow monstrously, destroying everyone in their paths. The rest of us, for the most part, and for the sake of our collective sanity, can only grin and bear it.

Today, however, is not one of those 'grin and bear it' days. I leave Lalang's office waving my index finger, unsure if it was indeed the right finger to shoot up when one cusses. I recall that there is a saying concerning showing someone a middle finger. It matters not, I think. It's easier for me to wave the index finger anyway; maybe I'm not cut out for this kind of language. But I don't think she even notices I'm waving the wrong finger. She has never been one to give much attention to detail anyway. A finger waved is a finger waved.

I was really tired of putting up WhatsApp profile statuses like, "I hope you step on a Lego" with the hope that she was nosy enough to check my profile pictures, and that she was sober enough to know that I had no other people than her in my life I would wish things like that on.

This I did as she called me in to talk about my coming late this morning. I never expected she could make such an issue of me having been ten minutes late, even though I spent five minutes just trying to get into the building because someone took their time with the security personnel as a considerable convoy formed outside the parking area. The ten minutes was apparently, in retrospect, the cause of her grumpiness when I greeted her in the morning.

The problem is that only Lalang qualifies as human enough to get stuck in traffic or have one of those chaotic mornings where the sock fairy wouldn't be the only one delaying the entire family. Only she has errands to run, and only she qualifies for occasional extended lunches, not to mention family responsibility leave. I'm so sick of her "I am the boss here" attitude.

I leave and stay in my space waiting for Lalang to follow me – not physically – but with a call or an email. I don't expect her to come storming into my "office," because I imagine her sitting there crying over a finger in the air. I work during lunch, deciding not to join the lunch group. Since yesterday's debate almost turned sour, I would really rather avoid the gang, especially since my own altercation with Lalang left my emotions in a rather unpleasant state.

The lunch topics can be in bad taste sometimes. It was so odd when Tholo suggested to Thabiso that he was living evidence that his parents had been, and probably still were, intimate. "I don't want to hear any of that stuff. My parents do no such things, and I'm no evidence of anything that happened at any time! You owe me one huge apology, and I'm not joining you here again until you can apologise and promise such gross topics would never be discussed again," Thabiso had said in irritation.

This unsavoury topic had come after Tholo's abuse of leave days was discussed. I had just laughed my guts out as Tholo, the renowned office joker, was telling us with the most cheerful of faces, that he was taking leave to attend to arrangements for his grandmother's funeral. Possibly his fourth granny to have passed away – and this excludes the two granddads that had already passed on. It wasn't clear why on the one hand he was aware that he had exhausted the natural number of granddads that could live and die, yet on the other he seemed to be having an endless list of grandmothers passing away.

What made the story funny, more than the number of grannies – which we're expecting would rise – was the expression on his face as he delivered the news, an expression that did not remotely correspond with the sad news at all. Tholo never bothered to explain that the grandmother perhaps this time around was a great aunt. No, it was always either his paternal or maternal gran. It is unclear why those that approved his leave were not asking any questions.

Four weeks earlier he took paternity leave for the birth of his firstborn child. The problem with this leave was that he took it based on a due date given by the sonar machine, which ended up changing, meaning that by the time he was due back at work, his wife had still not delivered. A few days later when an emergency C-section was confirmed, he needed to be at the theatre when "my wife would be cut here," he had explained pointing somewhere up there not far from his breast. I couldn't stop laughing.

It is amazing how God balances things out. Amidst hostile bosses there were always supportive friends, even crazy ones, who always ensured a healing dose of laughter to ease the tension and allow one to be productive without collapsing from the stress, I think as I walk quietly to the microwave oven to warm my lunch.

"If it's not the son of man Himself! The begotten – not made – son of Margaret and Mmusi," I hear Tholo shouting upon seeing Thabiso. I almost sprain my neck as I turn at lightning speed to face the voice that was spewing nonsense behind me! How could he be putting salt to an already open wound! Tholo never knows when to stop. Luckily Thabiso is slow to anger and does not, for the most part, take things personally.

It also helps to understand personalities like Tholo's, and I think Thabiso knows not to take him too seriously. *I am really glad I'm not joining them for lunch, I have had my unfair share of being today,* I say to myself again as I gobble the greens that have become one with my lunchbox. I will also be taking a break from them during my upcoming two-day break.

14

Anniversary leave

The conversations Makhananisa and I have when we both are on leave are just at another level. They're not like the rushed and exhaustion-fuelled, worried-about-the-week-ahead weekend conversations, nor are they like public holiday conversations.

Unlike other years, this year we decided not to go away for our tenth-year *marriage* – not wedding – anniversary. We opted to rather stay at home and enjoy what we seldom get to enjoy about our home. We're not going to do any house chores today. No, we make breakfast together and sit outside on the patio to enjoy the freedom of having absolutely nothing planned for the day. As we sit chatting and reminiscing over that first time we met, we drift towards a silly, light argument about who is luckier for having found the other.

"I am so special that a man had to lose a few years of his life just so he could end up finding me. I just wish you could, for once, grasp just how much God must have loved you to lead you in my direction, against all the odds. Honey, I'm such a treasure you had to lose so much in order to find me. What I know is that God so loves me that if any man was to be sent by him to be called my husband, he would have had to be tried and tested. This man was going to have to know without a shadow of a doubt how big a treasure he'd found. He would have to know that his life journey and all his travels and its many woes were to be thanked as they led him to his ultimate find – Precious Me!"

"You can be so vain, Virgo."

"Thank you, Pisces, now let's hear what you've got."

"I am such a big catch; you have no idea. You needed a realist like me to take you out of that childish romanticism of real love that you held in that pretty head of yours. And this realist is genuinely honest enough to be entrusted with that sensitive heart."

"Thank you for taking care of my heart, most of the time."

"Most of the time?"

"You cannot exactly say you have never made me cry?"

"Well, there you are correct," he says laughing as he pulls me closer. We sit silently, taking in the beauty of the moment and of everything around us. I take another look at the creativity surrounding us.

For the first time in months, I actually see the beautiful stretch of mountains, the colourful butterflies and birds that visit our butterfly bush, looking better acquainted with the surroundings than we are. I could sit here and watch nature the entire day – my entire life, to be honest.

They watch us as we watch them, probably wondering what it was these creatures found so fascinating. I look around and see houses at various stages of construction, and notice the different architectural designs and how all the colours seem to be in perfect harmony with each other, and with the environment.

I realise I had never seen all these things before. My eyes had merely hovered around and above them but have never truly seen. My brain must have been misinterpreting as noise the melodious tunes that the birds freely offered to my fatigued brain through my ears. My ears must have been fooled that I was actually listening but my brain, never.

How could anyone surrounded by so much beauty miss the inspiration provided by its energies? What I'm observing right now has always been here. But I have been absent. My mind has been filled to the brim by the crazy workplace I go to five days a week. "This cannot be right," I utter and have to explain to my husband what I was referring to. He has apparently been thinking along the same lines too.

It's amazing that Makhananisa and I do so many things that are similar. Sometimes I wonder whether he's not some long-lost twin brother of mine. I would be sitting in a particular pose and then catch him posing in exactly the same way. If I decide to buy bread on my way home from work, he would have decided to buy bread too. If I decided not to buy bread, we'll have no bread at home. Our kids even ask why we tend to buy takeaways on the same days. Our only problem is we seldom tell the other one that we are buying. It is a game our souls play, I suppose, one which we would rather just let be. I love the sync; it is magical.

"Do men feel the butterflies, though? I mean when you are in love and feeling loved – do you feel the so-called butterflies in your tummy as we ladies explain the feeling?"

"I'd love to think that we feel bees," Makahananisa says after a moment's pondering.

I briefly escape to that magical first time I fell in love with him. It was like nothing I've ever felt before. I could never have known that a simple, gentle stroke to my thumb could have so much power. That a possibly aimless gaze could make me so weak, rendering me helpless. If this was love, then those romantic comic books and my friends have all been right all along. I had been dismissing my friends' raves as exaggerations because how could their eyes light up so much when they talked about this thing? I have since found it, and I could give out raves that would make them crave.

I felt from the very moment I laid my eyes on him that he was my man. By the time he poured out his feelings I had known for some time already that we would be an item. Because I don't waste crushes. "Come on, Maki; he's crazy about you. Plus he is handsome. He is from a very well-respected family and has been raised very well. You'll be a fool to let him slip off," Rebabedi had told me in what seemed like an ad for this guy with a complicated name.

"But I have to wait for him to make the first move, Reba. I believe that men are hunters," I remember saying to my varsity friend. Though I liked him at first sight, and the knowing was there, some doubt was still present. That my friend seemed to know him fairly well was a good start, but I couldn't just take her word for it.

"Where have you drifted to, Mrs Mako?" asks my husband. It has been years since we've enjoyed sharing our first impressions of each other and our feelings back then. So I decide we will go to that beautiful place again. After all, it was that place where the foundation of our love was laid and cemented. And what a beautiful and strong foundation it is. I'm delighted he is in that revisiting-old-memories mood too.

"I recall how during one of my many tireless visits to your room before we hit it off, someone knocked at the door and you adjusted the hem of your dress. I thought to myself, 'this is a good sign; 'she's comfortable enough with me that she only has to adjust her dress when some other person knocks at the door.'"

And I insist my act was just an innocent reflex kind of thing, not conscious in any way, and devoid of any deep meaning. It had nothing at all to do with who was sitting next to me.

"Keep telling yourself that, Hun. I wasn't exactly wrong to think you were comfortable around me. You could already see us together. That much you have admitted."

"I recall how you had me in stitches when we started debating about how off-putting it was to see half-naked women advertising juice! And how the whole idea that women's bodies sold products was foolish and demeaning to women. I was surprised that you were more critical and I thought you were trying to impress me. So I argued that men are the whole reason naked women advertise juice and also the reason butts are now big business! If no one enjoyed seeing nakedness, then nakedness would not sell, period. Remember what your response was?"

"How could I remember? It's been almost two decades."

"Well, you remembered the hem-fixing incident!" I say, poking him slightly.

"I know what my views on that subject are and they have not changed one bit; that much I will get right. But I don't know what could have been funny at all. Besides, you are the one that has words and scenes engraved in your memory; so just go right ahead and remind me."

"Alright, alright. You said it didn't make sense that showing behinds, something everyone has, could get anyone interested in buying any product. And you added that there were a lot of people with disabilities in this world, but you have never come across or heard of any-one without buns. I just fell in love with your mind, your philosophy, and how you used language. That's why I can quote you so well."

"Yet you asked me the weirdest, sometimes most diffi-cult questions. Not to mention sometimes putting words in my mouth and claiming you could literally hear me saying the words."

"Unfortunately, the same memory sometimes becomes my worst enemy. Which is why you should always weigh your words and their possible long-term effect on both of us, before uttering them."

"Poor me."

"And you used to say 'if you don't know Maki, you have not met people."

"It's still true. I remember once when I came back from a relative's funeral at home, and you asked: "So, seeing that you attend so many funerals, what actually goes through your mind when you are there? Does anything at all?

"I responded by saying that I look around and wonder who among the many mourners will be next. 'That's it?' you asked, seemingly surprised. So I continued: No, it goes further than that, actually. I usually think: if I were to die of food poisoning later today as a result of the food I am about to eat, then this would have been my last Saturday alive. If I dropped dead today, next Saturday it would be my body being buried.

"Basically I was trying to tell you that I do think more about matters of life and death, and just how, as my uncle used to put it, 'we are walking corpses because death is always hovering over our heads.' But you had to shake my imagination up a bit. I will never forget what you told me concerning the imaginations that happen in this head," he says, massaging my temples a bit, prompting me to exhale.

I laugh. He was referring to that moment when I'd said to him: 'I wish that could be my worry, you really have it much easier – only thinking of your own mortality at funerals. I think about others' mortality too, and not in the way that you would imagine'.

"In my shaken pants, I assured you that I was listening. Scared in anticipation of what you were about to say," he says, shaking his head.

'And I almost fainted when you said: 'I have a curse of a gift. While you sit and wonder who is next in line, I know who is next. And I can somehow be strong at funerals because I get to think about death. I believe every death reminds us of our mortality. Because I think about dying a lot when I'm at the graveyards, I don't feel overwhelmed when my gift kicks in, and I start to see who was nearing death. But I tell you, walking through a mall and being shown whose bucket was about to be kicked is not a gift I would wish on anyone."

"Boy did I scare you!"

"To this day I don't know what I would have done had you not turned around and said you were pulling my leg!"

"I don't think you would have done anything at all. You had already concluded in that brilliant mind of yours that I was born to be your wife, to be Maki Mako!"

"Even you cannot argue with that. What other surname is there that's such a perfect match to your first name? It was all in the Master's plan, from when your mother thought she, somehow by herself, had chosen the perfect name for her new bundle of joy," he says, with the most unfitting romantic gesture I could have expected to wrap up such a statement. I guess, crazy in love we both are. Though far from over, this day has all the makings of a freedom day, a love day, a day well-spent.

I switch on my phone to find a message from Faith: "Sorry to disturb. Please call me when you have a moment. Nothing urgent. Maybe significant. Feeling 'bloated' and need to talk … Lol". I make the phone call. She wants to tell me about Collen's behaviour and that he seems to have been poisoned against her – probably against us. He'd just refused to do some simple admin task for Faith, a task he had been doing for everyone since his arrival.

"Don't mind him; he is being schooled. Remember I told you the other day that he said 'Lalang is dangerous' and seemingly made a turnaround as far as assisting me went? He has been abused and unlike us, cannot stand it. He had to finally squat and polish Lalang and Maphefo's behinds, in order to survive. His standing his ground and doing what was right was not serving him. Forgive him, he knows on what side his bread is buttered," I say as we wrap up our conversation.

We work with the strangest of people. I understand someone like Collen who is a young man full of hope; he is vulnerable to empty career promises made at the expense of his work ethics or humanity. But for people like Leonard to treat Faith and myself coldly whenever Lalang is around; and treat us warmly in her absence, that is just incredible!

"Maki, I can tell with absolute certainty whether or not Lalang is in the office, just by watching Leonard's attitude towards me," my mind replays Faith's words. "He would scream 'Hello' to me, and even come to me for small talk when Lalang is not around. But whenever she is in, I become invisible to him."

The extent people would go to appease others is really sad, I utter just as I catch myself putting the left shoe on the right foot. Then instead of switching one, I switch both the shoe and the foot and make the same mistake again. I laugh. They must never think they got me. This is called ageing. I am stress-free, and there is not a thing they can do about that.

15

Injured Behinds

My phone rings as soon as I put my bags down. I scramble for it and answer quickly without checking if it was a call worth taking, for fear of wasting time and losing the call.

"Good morning, may I speak to Miss Mo-g-wane, please?"

"It is Ms Mogwane speaking," I say emphasising the correct pronunciation.

"Hi Miss Mogwane, how are you this morning?" asks the telemarketer, referring to me by my maiden name and probably not expecting a truthful answer to the everyday greeting often cheated of its true purpose. I recognise the voice as the guy who has been calling me for some time now. The same one I have told over and over again, politely, that I was not interested at all in attending the investment presentation they would be making at my organisation in a few days' time. He has called and emailed a couple of times, never bothering to answer my question about where he obtained my personal details.

I have a nagging suspicion that someone in the organisation has either given or sold our details to this company. He had previously emailed and called on my office line saying they were coming here to give a presentation. They seem to have all my personal details; I wouldn't be surprised if they presented me with the name of my first pet. I am tired of being understanding now. I've just returned from the short leave that I wished wouldn't end, and I want to sit for a moment and recall the romantic time as I try to adjust to the unnatural office air.

"Do you really want to know how I am, Sir?" I ask politely, managing to crack a smile that would hopefully be felt across the wires, but without expecting an answer at all, as I continue.

Today, I will respond to the greeting as though he meant to ask how I was. If he was not really interested in knowing, then I would have to teach him to never again ask people how they were if all he expected was the usual, unconscious: "I am fine, thanks and how are you, Sir?" He is about to be told exactly how I am this morning! I hope he is up for it.

"I just arrived at the office out of breath because the elevators are out of order and I used the stairs all the way to the third floor. And you know how that can feel after a few days of relaxation, right? What's more, my supervisor who really thinks she is my boss though none of us owns this organisation, looked at me funny when I entered, as if I had absconded and did not earn my leave. Out there the traffic was just crazy this morning and my precious daughter whom I love so much told me she forgot her school project, and I had to make a U-turn after a three-kilometre drive. Can you imagine?"

"Oh, I'm sorry, Ma'am, but aren't those some of life's nicest problems ..?"

"No, that's not all. You know these radios how depressing they can be with the news they present to us. I cried my eyes out over a very sad story involving a family that was overcome with... I'd rather not even go there. My mother always said to me: 'My child; I truly believe that if you never shed a sincere tear for anyone in this life, then you are going to have to shed all your tears for yourself.'"

"We should be really thankful for having our comfortable lives."

"I suppose we should be. But what about those that have to endure all these hardships? Should we be grateful that it's not us but them? It doesn't sound right to me."

"No, that's not what I meant at all. They should be thankful too, for other reasons. In spite of our circumstances, we all have something to be grateful for. We should all appreciate those uncomfortable moments in time when we are practically being forced to know the true meaning of life. Now about my call, Ma'am, can you give me a minute to explain the reason for the call ..."

"Wait, I'm not done yet; I will give you a chance. I have to be honest about my state of being this morning. So, as if all that I already told you wasn't enough, I sprained my bum last night – my bum, Sir! And if you have ever wounded your rear end, you would know that buttocks aren't only meant for sitting. Damn, this pair is for standing, for walking, and for climbing the stairs, Sir. And crazy as it may sound, these two are for cooking and bathing too.

Every task that I normally accomplished without much thought required careful planning and delicate execution this morning because I had to accommodate my hurting behind. I could hardly believe the pain as I climbed those stairs. We take our abilities for granted, you know. Our behinds too. I mean when this injury occurred it only felt like a slight pull at my behind, nothing this crippling. So you would understand that ...

"... Hello, hello are you still there, Sir ... hello?"

He was gone. I don't think he ended the conversation on purpose. I really cannot allow my mind to go into that kind of negative thinking, especially since he seemed to enjoy the conversation. Pity I didn't even get to thank him for listening! I feel so much better after all that venting. He should have started with that other annoying intro:

"May I have a few minutes of your time to explain the reason for my call?" instead of asking how I am.

I feel a bit guilty that I did not give him a chance because we need to treat telemarketers well, you know, regardless of how many times they call after having been told 'no.' We all have to be relentless to survive. But sometimes they can be a pain in the behind, pun intended. I hope he never calls again because I would really hate saying no to him again, especially after having taken up so much of his time. I feel abused, though. Seriously, just getting to work has become so torturous.

Damn, there was still so much I could have complained about. So much to get off my chest! I could have vented on Sofia's behalf about black tax. It would have felt so good saying, 'I don't expect you to understand, Sir, but the version of black tax that some of us have to deal with is just out of this world. I mean when you left your parents' home and jetted off to varsity, it's likely your room was converted into that man cave your dad always wanted. Maybe even a second study because your room is on the sunny side of the house.

My friends and I, on the other hand, are busy building ourselves bedrooms at our parents' homes. And you're probably thinking that's voluntary or even crazy behaviour, aren't you? That we all need to be assisted in cutting the apron strings. I forgive you for not comprehending that we didn't grow up with a space we could call our own, but this was now our chance. And frankly, you don't know how much fulfilment you are missing out on! Not to mention the feeling of escaping to the countryside and spending holidays with family and old friends. Priceless!'

Maybe I should have complained to him about the beggars on that street corner who torment my spirit day in and day out. How is one to ever get over the look in that little boy's eyes as he knocks on your window asking for money? It tears at the soul. It's kind of like you are damned if you assist, and you're damned if you don't. I find my mind caught in between giving to the poor and not knowing for certain if someone – an innocent child or a disabled person – was being used against their will, to take a dig at our softer spots.

The other day the driver behind me hooted angrily when I succumbed to the torment and handed the boy a few coins. He was clearly disapproving because there were too many stories about the crimes behind street-corner begging. The poor kid could have been rented or trafficked. In any case, why wasn't he at school?

I'm torn into many pieces and pulled in several dark directions when I get confronted with a seemingly hungry child's pain. How would I ever know if the coins I sometimes holdback were to afford him a slice of bread? Or was it all going to his selfish monster masters? Besides, no matter how much any of us give, I doubt we could ever give enough to fix any beggar for life. Where would my giving end? It's a serious problem and torture to some of us — a continuous clash of wills.

Forget hurting behinds or the traumatising social ills that set me off to a bad start every day and please congratulate me for having made it to work in one piece this morning, Ms Lalang Masego! Congratulate me instead of watching that fancy watch of yours when I come through the door, like I am some irresponsible youngster. You have absolutely no idea what my mornings are like, so please give me a break. You've probably forgotten what it's like to have small kids. And while we're still on this topic, please, when I say I have to get my kids ready in the morning would you please stop saying 'we all have husbands!' That argument is tired now.

As I prepare to finally sit down for work, I'm mindful of the fact that I cannot afford to throw my buns on the chair mindlessly. I have to meticulously position the pair. I burst out in laughter as my thoughts drift to my grandmother's jokes about big behinds – her grandkids' big behinds, to be more precise. She used to tell us grandchildren how she had always loved to be overweight and that we've been blessed to be meaty. But the next minute grandma would make fun of us concerning the same body parts.

One moment she would be telling us that we can get away with creased clothing because as soon as our clothes graced our curvaceous bodies, the wrinkles would disappear. "They iron themselves out," she would say. But then someone with an even bigger behind would catch her eye, and she would say something like: "Seriously, you kids, do you mean to tell me that when you take a bath, your hands can actually reach your bums with such mountains of behinds? I really doubt that!" Where it concerned our behinds, grandma praised one minute and mocked the next. Much like Lalang's behaviour, only lighter and not at all hideous.

I giggle again as I agree with myself that behinds can be a very political topic. A memory flashes through my mental screen of a few years ago while travelling in Asia. My colleague and I had noticed some strange commotion around us. We hadn't realised that a few Chinese women were following us, seemingly in awe of our bums.

We turned to notice that the one woman must have walked a few blocks with us because we had seen her colourful attire earlier on, and she had been joined by several others that continued to point at our bums, completely in awe. Instead of taking offence, we chose to rather feel proud to be owning these assets, worthy of being fussed over. Maybe my upbringing and constant mocks from gran were preparing me for such moments. I owe it to her. I owe it to her that I can be so at peace with something that, to many, is such a delicate issue.

16

Manager vs. Leader

A Sepedi proverb says that *it is only mountains that will never bump into each other, yet with their shades even they sometimes do.* Who would have thought I would one day meet Amy? Amy – the name that greeted me that fateful day when I dared to step into Lalang land.

"Why isn't Lalang here? She needs this Emotional Intelligence course more than any of us here," Amy bluntly spurts out as soon as we exchange pleasantries over tea, and she learns I work with Lalang. This course is mandatory for all managers in our sector and Kaitlyn has been insisting that we all attend. I seize the opportunity and through a few giggles and say: "I'm so glad to meet a woman who has reported to Lalang. Finally, I can get some intelligence that could hopefully improve how we relate. How was your working relationship?"

Amy is happy to lay it all bare for me. She does not beat around the bush at all. "That madam Masego – I've never met anyone quite like her, in any way, shape or form. No one as cunning and devious. No one who can deceive with her soft voice while telling absolute lies and pretending to be caring. I've often wondered what kind of a man she was living with at home. If her behaviour at work is anything to go by, I doubt there is any peace in the Masego family home. I venture to say that no enlightened person could willingly spend their existence with such a person. But then again, Mrs Masego has a gift of switching personalities – or should I say a disease! She almost succeeded in damaging my self-esteem, that one. And for a while, she succeeded in putting a damper on my career." Teatime is over too soon, and Amy and I exchange contact details, just in case we don't get a chance to chat again.

"Me, if a person is good to me, I am good to them." My mind keeps unwittingly revisiting Lalang's introductory words to me because even a year later, they still make me feel uncomfortable. What time has provided, what it is known to provide, is a measure of clarity and understanding of what meaning lurked within the corners of that phrase. I was being groomed to do as she says, no matter what my convictions were. I am grateful to have met Amy, someone who was not only in the exact position I now find myself in but was a woman who felt bullied and misused by Lalang. I can see why Lalang would have likened me to her. Was she looking for another Amy to bully when she recruited me? I will never know.

Like a tape with a scratch, my mind goes on and on, replaying some famous sayings from Ms Lalang, that, unlike many quotable quotes, are as bitter to digest as they are to swallow. "I have serious concerns because it doesn't seem as though we're on the same page..." I hold my head in a fruitless attempt to stop the tapes from playing. I'm enjoying the Emotional Intelligence course so much, but I feel cheated out of it because my mind is divided. Why am I allowing her to remotely control me?

I take a deep breath and finally put the salt that is Lalang on the right shelf to be pulled out at a later stage. It works. My head would not agree to let it go, but it agrees to put it on hold to be regurgitated on later.

I feel light as air as I scan the packed room hoping to catch sight of Amy as the session closes. A message pops up on my phone. "It was lovely meeting you, Maki. Unfortunately, I have to rush home now. Let's keep in touch."

Why are we lacking so often in this type of intelligence, though? I throw the question at the forming rain clouds as I walk through the light wind to my car. So many employees seem to be experiencing some form of abuse from the workplace. How are we to remove these obstacles to service delivery and fighting poverty if some of us refuse to see any value in acquiring these softer skills? I cannot do anything about the fact that my manager isn't here to listen to how far empathy goes; to learn about its far-reaching impact and its place in our very bottom line.

I sigh. As a drive off, the air catches volume and the lightness I had felt earlier slowly disappears. It would appear that all the weird and terrible things Lalang ever said to me are being scrutinised in my brain, sadly not for the first time. Lalang is under judgment based on her words. Oh, how I wish the judgment carried some punitive measures! Unfortunately, the only punishment there was, was being received by me, myself and I. The same wounding words I would prefer to scrap from my memory have found permanent space in the fragility of my soul. I have allowed them to have an immortal power to give me almost the same sinking feelings of powerlessness they had when they were uttered. Kudos to Lalang for getting so much return on her miserable investment. I lose tons of respect for Lalang every time the words are brought back to my memory.

I sometimes think I have learnt to accept her infamous utterances and nasty looks and given them the recognition they demand because I was working with an uncaring, confidence-busting, and peace snatcher of a woman. But I still find myself lamenting over the things that I have to get used to in order to survive. There is a lot that still requires getting used to. Certain realities, though still surprising, I have managed to make peace with over the months. Like the fact that Maphefo was going to do what Maphefo wanted to do. More appropriately, that Lalang had a crony in Maphefo, and there wasn't a damn thing any of us could do about that. No need crying over spilt milk. A girl has to do what a girl has to do. Having nourished my spirit with some coping strategies and emotional intelligence, I am determined not to let Lalang or her far-reaching words get the better of me. But the determination is nothing new.

The sound of an ambulance siren answers my question about whether the crawling traffic was a result of an accident, a stuck or slow moving vehicle, or maybe just some traffic officers going about their business. Amazing how terrified we are of the uniformed men and women. Even on a freeway, many of us instantly slow down to 40km at the sight of the traffic police. That is how the well-intending officers cause traffic, whether or not they are aware of it.

Three ambulances and a fire truck pass by before I can wrap up the traffic officers' story in my head. At best, someone is sadly not sleeping in their bed tonight. I let out a big sigh as my thoughts drift to my favourite couch and blanket and my double cream yoghurt. I slap myself guiltily and start thinking of my husband and kids instead. I would really hate for my kids to receive devastating news about me when all their young minds were assured of was that mommy would soon be home. "Lord, please save the people involved in this seemingly terrible accident," I manage to pray.

I'm distracted by the sight of a pension-age white man wearing a formal white shirt, sitting on a wooden fence by the park, staring at the walking-pace traffic. I see him as a retired professional who is either looking at the traffic to remind himself just how lucky he was to be out of the rat race, or a man bored out of his mind, wishing he could have been the one stuck in traffic on his way from work. I need to hear his story. My curiosity and yearning for human interaction get the better of me and without giving my second voice any chance to say no, I decide to pull off the road, scared of not following my instincts to do so, and possibly wondering later what might have happened had I followed it. The traffic is still heavy anyway, and maybe it would have subsided by the time I get back on the road. *Let me rather do something useful with my time.*

Fear engulfs me as I slowly approach the elderly man, who was also looking at me in wonder and anticipation. What mood will I find him in, I wonder. What crazy ideologies does he hold? What if he is a die-hard racist who cannot relate at any level with dark-skinned members of the universe and would not welcome my act of acknowledgment of his humanity? Oh my goodness, what if he is mad and he starts chasing me like the bum who threw my food parcel back at me in anger last week? *I can be so naïve and trusting sometimes – too much of a chance-taker,* I think with my mother's voice instead of my own. I stay frozen for a moment before I could manage to take another step forward.

Slowly I walk, realising with every step I take just how vulnerable I was. I reach for the car keys in my pocket so they can hold my hand and balance my steps during this trying moment. And then I quickly pull my hand out of my pocket as I imagine the old man shooting me in self-defence because, of course, I was drawing a gun out to shoot at him. I'm in too deep now; I have to keep walking. I really need to find out what thoughts are occupying that grey head as it looks at the traffic. No, I have to find out, or I will forever regret.

"*Goeiemiddag, Meneer,*" I greet him in his presumed language to hopefully warm him up.

"*Môre, môre my kind,*" he responds cheerfully saying "morning, morning, my child." Shoulders can now go down. He is at the very least approachable.

I've mastered the greeting, but I have to switch to English now.

"This may sound strange to you, but I happened to notice how you stared at the passing traffic ... and I started wondering what thoughts could be going through your wise head as you looked at the rush hour being turned into a chameleon's race. I thought instead of asking myself, I should just come and find out from you. I knew that one way or another, I'd learn something," I manage to say, not sure if I was even making any sense at all.

"You are such an old soul, such a sweetheart kind; are you an angel perhaps?" the oldie asks with a twinkle in his eye and a smile as he continues.

"Not many your age would take the time to sit with an old rag like me — not many. Many young people look at us as though we have nothing to offer them. Many forget they too will be old one day, and it comes quicker than we think. To the youngsters, ageing is something that we old ones deserve. We have brought it onto ourselves. And don't get me wrong, child, I love my age and I would not change these golden years for anything. My sitting here is part of my afternoon ritual. Maybe you've never noticed me in the rushing madness, or maybe it's because I sit at different places and at varying times."

"By the way, my name is Maki. Maki Mako."

"Very pleased to meet you, child; my name is Peter, but you may call me Ngwato," he says again with a twinkle in his eye as he stretches his hand toward my outstretched one. I am more than impressed with this chap. Not only is he welcoming but he also has an African name to boot. He explains that the name, a praise name, was given to him by his former colleagues because of his love for all things African. I close my eyes and thank my spirit for having not wielded to my fears of opening up to this stranger who was very quickly becoming a friend. We exchange contact numbers and I prepare to rejoin the traffic, which was becoming lighter by the second.

"Thank you, Maki *ngwana'ka*, may you and your family be blessed. I assure you that you did not lose a moment's time by pulling out of the traffic. The car that was in front of you, you will see somewhere ahead, and you would be in the same place and time you would have been had you stayed in the traffic all this time."

I smile at the truthfulness of his words. I've often noticed how the car that speeds up past all the others, sometimes nearly causing an accident, would be with us at the next traffic lights. Life is balanced like that.

"I will be in touch and will be sure to stop every now and then when I see you."

"And when you cannot stop, just hoot and wave," he says as I leave, evidently having enjoyed the strange company. Oh, how much of the day's weight I have shed during the ten minutes or so with my brand new friend, Uncle Ngwato!

"So you always strive to take well-considered decisions and are always careful not to take a wrong turn? How do you assure yourself you are making the absolute correct decision?

"Have you ever changed lanes in traffic because the next lane was moving and the one you were in was slow, only for the latter to start moving as you switch, and the one you joined starts to crawl? Has the same happened at the supermarket pay point? See, my child, many flying cars have arrogantly passed my shocked behind, and many of them I'd caught up with waiting on a traffic light ahead.

I tell you, I've even passed such flying cars as my lane would mysteriously start to move as theirs got stuck. It is not who is the fastest that counts; it is best to walk than to run." I replay my conversation with Uncle Ngwato; his wise lessons, which he repeated in different ways during our short chat, ringing in my ears.

My own grandmother used to say: "If you run, you better not fall because a runner falls the hardest. Walk! The destination will be there, waiting; it is not going anywhere". There has to be some level of truth to this — a truth I probably need to keep close to my heart every day.

17

More working mom blues

"Mama," my son says in a rather responsive tone. He must have heard my spirit calling out his name. It happens quite often. I would be thinking about saying something to one of my kids, and they would respond, having somehow heard me calling their name. I sometimes wonder if there might be any possibility at all that I had unconsciously called their name, not in my head but out of my mouth. But most times I'm certain I didn't.

This is one of those times because Motheo responds as he lays his ailing head against my shoulder after an episode of gentle combing. He does this often as he cringes from the pain of being combed, no matter how gentle. Today is different because he is not feeling well.

It's a very difficult thing for any mother to have to send your child to crèche or school when they're not feeling well. Most mothers, especially working mothers, have had to deal with the dilemma at some point in their lives – together with the pain and the associated guilt. I know that the five extra minutes I give him to lie in my embrace might result in me being fifteen minutes late, which Lalang will be happy to angrily point out as disrespect.

On any other day, I might have felt penitent for being late. Not today. Not when my child's well-being is involved. But today I have a meeting and a presentation to make. "I will make sure to come back and take you to the doctor as soon as the meeting is over, okay?" I reassure Motheo as I give him pain medication. I cannot let him see just how stressed I am. But the symptoms are those of kiss' syndrome because once the fever subsides, he becomes a healthy child until the medication wears off. Two hours, that's all I need, and I will be back with him.

I know they will remind his dad at crèche that bringing a sick child is not good for the rest of them. But hey, he too must have picked up the bug from there because none of us at home have it. The control measures cannot be a hundred percent effective. I can only hope that Daddy doesn't succumb to the pressure and bring him back home. If he does that, he'll have to stay with him.

Look at just how time flies in the morning. I sit and do a little thinking and then I'm on the verge of being seriously late and possibly also on the receiving end of a lecture on the working hours policy, or nasty stares if I'm lucky. I drag my anxious body to the bathroom for a quick shower. My mind drifts to Neverland yet again, as I sit on the bed staring at my dress. You see, I've become so uncomfortable with this 'working for a living' and 'reporting to bosses' thing that Neverland has become accustomed to my impromptu visits.

The trouble with these visits is that they seldom occur on a weekend or holiday, they are notorious for creeping up on me when I'm running out of time on weekday mornings. Surprisingly, that's when I enjoy them the most, for they offer a very welcome escape from my reality. Without them, who knows where I would be? Maybe I would be in a mental institution suffering from depression, or worse in jail, having choked someone in anger. Drifting is my lifeline. Without it, I would never have started asking myself some hard questions about my life and whether I was living it as my creator so lovingly intended. I wouldn't have been financially savvy enough to live frugally, pay off all debts, including the bond, invest in property; and I certainly wouldn't have started investing at a relatively young age. I have come to believe that God loves me so much that He makes working for a living a bit uncomfortable for me so that I would pursue his will for my life. If all was hunky dory at work, I might have remained complacent and might not have strived to follow my dreams and realise my purpose in life. I will forever be grateful to those that have caused me discomfort and made it difficult for me to be a happy employee. I'm grateful to them because one of these days I will get to work having had enough of it all to finally sign that resignation letter, which has been sitting nicely in a file inside my office cupboard ever since I started working with Lalang.

Someone knock some sense into me now, I say to myself as I swallow what's left of my pride and approach the unapproachable woman to wish her a happy birthday. I opt to forget that a couple of months earlier she failed to acknowledge mine even as two colleagues made some noise and sang 'happy birthday' as I entered the office. I shall forgive and forget. Maybe she was going through a tough time that particular day; one would never know. I'm growing to learn not to be quick to judge. Besides, I don't need any bad energy today. Not only did I send my sick child to crèche but I have a presentation to deliver, and I need the atmosphere to be positive. I'm already distracted by thoughts of possible calls I might miss from the crèche.

"I don't agree with you at all," a familiar voice slices through the silent room, straight to my nerves. My heart stops and jumps at the same time when my eyes confirm it's indeed the voice of the one with whom I've had the discussion on this topic — the very one who is supposed to shield and support me. I gather my crumbled confidence and vow on my great-grandmother's feisty name that my spirit shall not be broken. Not this time. Not in this manner. If she was not willing to bolster my idea - the very one she had agreed with until this moment - I will do so myself. I will be damned if I let her get away with her ill-intended comment. The saying 'being thrown under the bus' suddenly makes sense as I realise it was going to be one long morning.

"Wait a minute, aren't you colleagues?" I feel a little relief as this question is raised by one attendee, who is visibly confused about the open disagreement and attack launched by Lalang. Of course we're colleagues, and the lady knows that all too well. Until this moment I was oblivious to the shock on people's faces and the nasty stares some delegates direct at Lalang. I had thought she was winning. But people could see what she was trying to do and were not impressed by the stunt she pulled.

"Ms Masego and I are colleagues, yes. I report to her. I believe all of us present here have the same intention - to share ideas that we envisage will have a positive impact on the masses out there. Those ideas need to be probed as extensively as possible so that they can be implemented with the same vigour with which they were developed. As a unit, we have discussed this early warning system and expressed similar enthusiasm about it. On the concept I think we agree, no doubt about that. But our ideas are not cast in stone. We are here to consult, after all," I say, trying to save the embarrassing situation where our audience witnessed a manager attacking a subordinate in an open consultative meeting.

I give the cold shoulder as Lalang tries to address me with a smile as though nothing had happened. How could we agree a hundred percent on an idea one minute, and then totally hold different views the next? "You know what, Lalang, save it! I tried to act professionally because that's just who I am – not because you were right, or because I'm scared of you. Now go take a long walk on a short pole; I have an ill child to pick up at crèche," Ntsobe unexpectedly utters as we gather our belongings and I head straight home to attend to Motheo. She thinks I did not notice that she only smiled because people were congratulating me on a great presentation! She will find me ready for her tomorrow, alright! I am sick of it all!

If she thinks that she was sending a message to me when she told me she would one day beat Kaitlyn to a pulp because she used to beat up girls like her, she has another thing coming. I might not be as experienced as she is, but I will not allow her to walk all over me.

The music saves my heart as I get swallowed by the open road. At least something was going well today. I will be with my baby in no time. I throw all thoughts of Lalang and traces of bitterness out into the wind as I drive. Maybe they will arrive at the throne of God as a prayer for me to be saved from this mess.

18

The softer edges

I have no appetite for this ageing thing. If this is how it feels like to have a lousy flu when you are forty, then I only have a craving for the cradle, nothing beyond.

I wake up from a two-hour long self-sedated rest, wondering what might possibly have happened to my body as I laid down my bones. I feel pains and sensations in parts of my body the existence and importance of which I've never had to waste my time on. Today those parts are teaching me that they too deserve my attention, but more so, they're teaching me that not one inch of my body is without, at least, some menial function.

I reach for my phone, not expecting a response from Lalang, but I find one today. "Noted," says her cold response to the message I sent two hours earlier to inform her of my health state and the fact that today was not one of those days I could drag my body to the office. The boy had passed the bug my way. At least she responded today, even though she was careful not to sound caring.

I wonder as I unbundle myself to walk to the bathroom if her somewhat humane act of acknowledging my message today could be a sign that I was dying. I stare intensely at my reflection in the mirror as I wash my hands, examining any signs of life or near-death in my eyes, which appear even smaller. Other than their shrunken state, they look even brighter than the sun itself. I'm still filled with life, after all. I smile. It has to be about her having done some sort of introspection or something to that effect.

Having arrived at that conclusion, I concentrate more on my movements – every lift and step of my foot, and every inhalation and exhalation, and how I feel and sound as I breathe and move. My body does everything on its own all the time without my aid or acknowledgment of just how it interacts with itself for me to be able to simply lift a leg or think of thinking about something. I don't know why all of a sudden I think my insignificant self was capable of controlling or managing it. Maybe I should acknowledge the master processes more.

As I slide back under the blankets, I resist the temptation to pick up my phone and send Lalang a sarcastic 'thank you for wishing me well' message. No, I can do with some positivity today.

As I relax, I feel my body almost being lifted in the air, and my forehead being hit by a heat flush that leaves me wondering whether I was having a heart attack.

I hear Thabiso's voice saying as it often says, "don't give illness the upper hand by being cooped up in bed. Stand up; you are too blessed to be sick". I then hear another voice reminding me of the belief we held as kids that if you sleep too much when you're feeling unwell, you might just wake up to find that you were no more.

I get up and make myself breakfast and flush it down with a colourful dessert of a home-made concoction and fever meds. "I will live," I think out loud as I carefully slouch on the couch to watch television, happily leaving my body and my day to unravel as they would. As they were meant to.

Everyone has a softer side, I believe. There are very few people in the universe that are completely bad. The born evils and the downright evil are a rare species. But can we really say we know without a shadow of a doubt that someone was born that way? This belief makes me give undeserving people the benefit of the doubt sometimes. That is not to say I am naïve, though. I never do this at the expense of my well-being. I guess it has more to do with looking at someone and asking myself what struggles they might be going through for them to be so bad.

I sometimes cannot help but look at Lalang in that light. My husband's theory is that Lalang has an annoying monkey on her back that keeps scratching her, and this is the reason she can do such awful things with not a drop of shame. Her soft-spoken nature is just a cover-up. Faith has told me this many times before too.

I know by the frequent repetition of "if you do not know her, you could find yourself melting up as you listen to her while deluding yourself about how peaceful and sweet this woman is," that Faith herself could never quite get used to Lalang's deceptive tone and destructive undertones. I bet, like me, she sometimes finds herself wanting to give the woman a chance, only to be reminded that you do not dare wrap up a snake in a blanket and think it will sleep peacefully, dream good dreams and wake up to thank you with a warm embrace. If the embrace was to be there, it would be calculated and fatal. With the likes of Lalang, every move is deliberate and full of intent. And most often than not, the intent is for the subject's destruction.

She is consistently most deceptive in two scenarios: when she pretends to care about our challenges and when she talks about how frustrated she is with Kaitlyn, her manager. By Faith's admission, Lalang almost deceived her into disliking Kaitlyn. She soon realised that whenever Lalang would open her mouth to talk about Kaitlyn, it was to criticise her, be it about the granny clothes she apparently wears, how much of a know-it-all she is, or how terrible her management style is. The criticisms often extend to Kaitlyn's close friend, Lilly, about whom Lalang says she wants to vomit whenever she lays eyes on her. Lalang is deceptive because when she is around these individuals, she is their sweet angel. She has managed to poison Maphefo against a lot of people, and now Maphefo cannot say anything good about anyone. In fact, as far as Maphefo and Lalang are concerned, nobody in the organisation is good at anything. Nobody but the two of them, of course. The ear-cracking laughter and talk of how stupid and undeserving of their high positions many people are, feed their existence.

The danger with people like Lalang is that they have grown to be so great at gossiping and lying that they cannot help themselves. A wise person would know that the way she gossips about others to them is the same way she gossips about them when they're not there.

I'm not certain whether my colleague Leonard is completely unaware of Ms Masego's character and her lying nature, or if he just enjoys believing her. My thoughts revisit what Lindi told me the day before.

Apparently, Leonard was talking about how Ms Masego is so angry because I did not do some work that she asked me to do. I was taken aback. If there was any work I was supposed to have done and didn't do, surely there would be some follow-up communication regarding that work.

One could easily sue the likes of Ms Masego one day. She also lied about Faith's studies, telling Leonard that Faith has failed the post-graduate course she pursued last year, yet Faith had passed, with flying colours to boot. I'm reminded of my child's preschool teacher telling parents, "if you choose to believe everything your kids say about us teachers, then we'll also choose to believe everything they tell us about you." Maybe Leonard is a poor judge of character and doesn't know that Ms Masego talks about him too, but some of us, having figured her lying tendencies, choose to take everything with a pinch of salt, and sometimes we add hot sauce too.

19

Village tranquil

I did not hear my cousin, Dibuseng, knocking until she started screaming in her characteristic squeaky voice. Every time I find myself during a normal working day in the village where I grew up, I marvel at the easy, simple, stress-free life that village people, including some of my old friends, are living. I'm on leave and have, as I often do, chosen to visit my parents and spend two nights enjoying the serenity of village life.

I lose track of time as I watch in admiration and envy as one of the neighbours sweeps her front yard, occasionally stopping to exchange greetings with a passer-by followed by small talk that embraces everything and nothing. It's no wonder village people have so much goodwill; they are content with what little they may have in the way of material possessions and are generally not stressed.

As Dibuseng comes in, my mind travels swiftly to the office block where I work as I attempt, in vain, to put one world alongside the other. Which one is better? I throw the question to the air and watch it dissipate as the dust from all the front yards that were being swept fight for their own space too.

I visualise the usual turmoil at the office and see stress levels higher than Mount Kilimanjaro. For a moment I pity those I see at work through my mind's eye, forgetting just how temporarily outside that space I am. I opt to forget this is just for the time being and allow my head to enjoy the view from outside as I return to the office environment. I see dedicated servants of the people, working their behinds off on some project that, depending on how the birds were singing, might just end up good. But continue they will. Against all the odds, crippling circumstances, and hostility all around them, they continue.

I hear Mr Sebelebele greeting everyone with his customary Monday morning greeting: "*Ja*, we have conquered another Monday. Just by being here this morning we are victors. Many have tried but were denied by certain bottled drinks. The week will soon be dust under our feet".

Mr Sebelebele is an incurable optimist. He is the type of guy that three weeks into January, would remind everyone just how close the December holidays were. "January is almost over and at this rate, well, it's done, the year is gone," he would say.

My own traditional broom in hand, I have forgotten that I was supposed to be rushing to beat the sun coming out. No one can stand that sun's blazing heat, so everyone rushes the outdoor jobs lest it comes out and burn their complexions away. Young women cover almost every inch of their bodies with clothes to escape sunburn. A few even look like they have traded complexions, for suddenly their beautiful dark or brown skins have turned pale.

The exercise itself makes me sweat a river. *Who needs a gym membership?* I think to myself. A moment after I've bent over, I have to get upright again and respond to a greeting from another neighbour. It's a welcome break as my waist, and lower back already felt the pinch. The breaks come in quite frequently.

My cousin just happens to find me in too deep a thought. I worry that I was that absentminded. What if I did not hear someone pass a greeting? It doesn't take much in the village to be labelled as 'self-important' if you don't greet or return greetings. In the company of Dibuseng, I quickly forget about what others might have thought as she starts occupying my mind with her silly jokes.

I'm glad she came just as I was about to finish sweeping. We sit ourselves down on the wooden bench and immediately start sharing news about our lives. Both my cousin and my sister Modiegi are teachers. They're on their mid-term school break while I am only getting a taste of their enviable lives for two days. Whenever the two of them are together, laughter is inevitable. We sit and share all the work stories, and they are as horrid, as unbelievable and as funny as it comes.

Dibu tells us about a colleague of hers who was so fed up of his unappreciative manager in whose eyes he could never do anything right. The guy was apparently so defeated he was even saying he would be happy getting a job at an immigration office or post office or anywhere where he could be assigned the task of stamping lifeless papers.

His cognitive decline had been the subject of jokes at work, thanks to bullying colleagues. His manager led the crazy pack by telling him in a meeting that his job would henceforth be that of binding files. The guy gracefully accepted his binding job, but his dream job still remained stamping where he could get to take his frustrations out on papers and tables.

"It would be exactly the kind of demotion I would wish for someone like our know-it-all selfappointed manager of a colleague, Maphefo. But I do get this guy wishing this demotion on himself. Frankly, I would be more content hitting papers on tables all day than I could ever be working with Lalang. Boy, would I slam the living daylights out of those papers! I can almost feel the stress levels dissipate just thinking about how hard I would hit those papers and how productive I would be. A thousand times better than being in that unhealthy office and working with those people," I say to much laughter. They don't realise how honest I'm being.

"I would imagine placing that Lalang and them in between paper and table as I smash," Dibu adds. In spite of how much I dislike working with them, the thought of smashing them makes me feel repulsed. I'm glad I still have some soul left in me.

Modiegi thinks she will lose her mind because she carries the problems of her school, her country and of the world on her small shoulders. She worries about the state of affairs where it's everyone for himself, where professionals seem to have forgotten the ethos of their professions. A state of affairs where patients could die because a civil servant needs a double-digit increase, a situation where a lot of people seem to have lost respect for life.

"Just last week a trainee teacher told me straight to my face that she doesn't have to work because this is the government. Where does a graduate get such scary ideas? What are we teaching our kids?"

I neutralise her anger by assuring her that the trainee's view was an isolated case because I have mentored a few hard-working, committed, smart interns in the past. They were driven, and while they were aware of the situation in the country, they showed enough hope, drive and ambition to make their impact. But I've also heard of youngsters who think they are so educated they deserve to enter the job market at the top.

"These days one is scared even to mention that one is a public servant. While a few people acknowledge that there are some hard-working and committed servants who give their best to the betterment of this country, many others are happy painting all with the same brush. Who could blame them, though? Aren't we all subjected on a daily basis to mediocrity?"

I share more about my own chameleon of a manager who seems to forget, at the drop of a hat, her fiduciary duty. A manager who is so eager to bend the rules to accommodate those close to her, even if it means wasteful expenditure.

I tell them about a particular incident when Lalang, rightfully, expressed her disapproval of people wanting to stay over at a hotel for a conference that was being held less than seventy kilometres away from town. "We cannot allow people to sleep over at the conference venue; they must drive back even if it is late at night," Lalang had ordered. "Who wants to stay over?" She thought to ask.

"Maphefo," Faith responded. None of us could have anticipated Lalang's swift change of demeanour as soon as Maphefo's name was mentioned.

"I suppose if people want to sleep over they can do so. *Ja*, plus we need to spend a little bit ... we are not doing well on the expenditure front, and I don't want to have to account for why we did not spend," Lalang said, switching gears the moment she heard the request to spend a night at the relatively nearby expensive hotel, was made by her crony, Maphefo. Lalang approves unreasonably long stays for Maphefo. At one point, a three-day trip was planned for Maphefo and an intern for a meeting that lasted two hours. The pair left on a Sunday evening for a meeting on Monday at 10am. Instead of flying the one hour back after the short meeting, they slept over again, using the afternoon and the next morning to shop before flying back in the afternoon.

"So, she's not even a great financial manager either? In which management area does she excel? I cannot believe she would be so wasteful of the taxpayer's money, spending just to give the false impression that she is productive!" Modiegi remarks in disbelief.

"And most of these trips Faith and I only get to know about either by observing Maphefo's absence or watching her and her accomplice wheeling their luggage out of the office. Lalang loves keeping us in the dark."

"I thought this Maphefo girl reports to you. Shouldn't you at least know her whereabouts?"

"There was a time last year when Lalang took her on a trip without my knowledge or approval as her line manager. No one said a thing. I just noticed their absence from the office. I sent a message to Maphefo to ask about her whereabouts, and for two days she ignored my messages and didn't take my calls.

After a couple of days, they came back, and I asked Maphefo to explain why she was out of the office without permission. She then arrogantly told me she went on this trip at Lalang's instruction. After this incident, Lalang immediately started hinting that everyone was going to have to report to her in order for performance to improve". We are familiar with the codes.

"And those rumours about stolen funds, was there ever an investigation?"

"My dear, an investigation was spoken about, but it did not succeed because Lalang quickly wormed herself into the executives' hearts, and she succeeded in sweet-talking them and showing her best side while backbiting other people."

I cannot comprehend how people can happily feed their kids with stolen money. With blood money! I don't think they themselves know what they are doing. I mean, if money was not meant for me, obviously someone else would have been cheated of it, and they would, therefore, be in pain. Their kids would be in pain too.

What sort of animalistic moron gets to think it's okay for their own kids to be happy while another person's kids were unhappy, all because of them? What makes it okay for us to interpret hustling in such a dog-eat-dog and 'everyone for themselves' manner?

"If you hear her talking about how Kaitlyn used to keep the staff in her office until the wee hours, doing nothing, just so she could claim for overtime and how she, Lalang, finds Kaitlyn's behaviour despicable, you would think she was clean herself."

I pause to notice Dibuseng concentrating on the watermelon she is savouring. "Hmm, the level of attentiveness you give to your food, Dibuseng. I tell you if you could give even half as much attention to that man of yours as you give to your food, he would be eating from the palms of your hands."

Without intending to, I had prompted my cousin to start talking about her husband, whom she mockingly refers to as 'the Pope' because he loves making himself scarce around the home.

"I would do anything to find out what Melvin does with his money, you know. I always knew him as a miser who bought meat every day and never allowed any extra meat in the fridge, but these days he has graduated to a complete epic level that would make him pitiable even by Satan himself."

"Why?" I ask with interest.

"He has stopped buying meat altogether. One day I served him pap without any meat just to spite him. I put it in a covered plate on a tray and laid a fork and knife for him. I'm still shocked when I think about what happened when I gave him the food."

"What happened? Did he throw it away?"

"No. He asked for some spices and ate the whole darn serving of pap with a mixture of chicken spice, tomato sauce, and cayenne pepper. He did not complain at all and continued acting as though all was well throughout the evening. I gave up the battle on that day."

We delve deeper into both our working and married lives. We talk about the challenges and connections we make at work. But mostly, we lament the connections we have come short of making.

"I read somewhere that when a man does this kind of thing, it may suggest that either something is going on at home ... or maybe something isn't going on at home," I light-heartedly remark as I know Dibuseng wouldn't be injured. And true to her nature, she bursts out laughing.

"I know what you're not saying, Cuz. You know people like spontaneity. But spontaneity will excite you at first, and then it will begin to hurt you, slowly causing your marriage to disintegrate."

My childhood friend Prudence puts a punch on our interesting conversation and veers us in a completely different one as she enters, skilfully balancing a bucket full of water on her head while carrying a baby on her back and pushing another in a wheelbarrow inside a plastic bathtub with some clothing.

I freeze and cross my fingers that she won't miss a step and hurt one of the kids with the load on her head. I remind myself that there was nothing scary about the balancing act and that I have never heard of anyone getting injured that way. But I still cannot just sit and watch her offload and sit, so I stand and assist her with the bucket and take the baby off her back.

I have heard about Pru's separation and ensuing divorce from her high school sweetheart. She had kept it a secret from me. I was not sure whether she kept it from me because by telling me, she would be admitting to having been unhappy in her marriage, or she was just afraid I would be disappointed or terribly hurt at the end of a marriage, the roots and branches of which I knew so well? She knew that I thought her marriage to be the happiest of marriages. Was she living a lie?

"Why did you not tell me, Pru?"

"Remember how I told you about his never admitting to his farts, ever?"

"Yes, we joked about that a couple of times."

"The truth is, his denying that he farted, every time without fail, made me trust him less and less. I wondered what else he lied about if he could lie about something as airy as a fart. Each time he farted and denied it, he really made me mistrust the other denials I've heard from him. It made me see him more and more as a liar and the more I analysed things this way, the less truthful he seemed in other areas too."

"You are actually divorcing your husband based on a fart? You're leaving him because he lies about his farts?"

"No, darling. I'm divorcing him because he's a lying old fart. The more he disowned the farts, the smellier they got and the smellier they got, the more disgusted I became with him and his farts.

The farts and his lying about them are really just a metaphor for our lives together. They kept reminding me just how many denials I've encountered and just how little I truly knew about the truths behind those denials. For if he can look me in the eye and deny a mere fart, one that I'm certain was his, what else is he lying about?"

"But what if he only denied the farts because he was ashamed to be farting in your presence? You know what they say: a king does not fart in front of the queen and vice versa," I say, mindful of the fact that our conversation had cut out Dibu and Modiegi, who sit listening like school pupils afraid to interrupt the teacher. Totally unlike the two of them.

"Ashamed? After more than a decade together? This is a guy who is ashamed of very little ... he is capable of much more disgraceful things," Pru says matter-of-factly.

I nod in agreement. Still, I cannot understand where this four month old she is carrying on her back came from if they separated a year ago. He's a spitting image of Pru's soon to be ex-husband, Morwalo. I don't ask. She will tell me all about it one day.

Village life always affords me a fresh new set of eyes with which to view my life – or city life in general.

The stresses of my job can make one look at a woman like Pru and admire, even envy, the simplicity and serenity of her life in spite of everything she must be thinking she doesn't have.

I start to think just how one could easily leave it all and go off the grid in the village. I'm sick of the unreciprocated love and sweat because a lot of the stuff we work for isn't working for our well-being at all. I would hate to look back at my life one day when I'm old and regret that I spent so much of it as a slave. There certainly are no beggars to be found in this simple life, and that alone makes the village desirable.

I rest my head on a pillow as my sister and I continue chatting, not expecting to doze off, nor to fall into any daylight dreams. By the pit toilets at the corner of my parents' yard, two snakes are crawling away, crossing the loose wire fencing to the yard next door. They are greyish in colour, and they seem to have a scaly appearance that causes blood to rush speedily through my body, both in terror and disgust. To my surprise, they also appear to be injured on their backs. They're crawling away slowly, and I watch them go.

It seems to have taken only a few minutes for me to fall asleep, dream and wake up to the sound of Dibuseng's voice as she announces that she managed to find a tasty-looking watermelon from the shop. I am still nauseated by the dream, and I dismiss the ladies' insinuations that only a pregnant version of me would ever let a watermelon pass.

None of it makes any sense even to me. I am not the vomiting type, not even during pregnancy. But here I was being so nauseated by a dream I just had, I have no stomach left at all for my favourite thirst-quencher!

"It means those witches have finally been defeated. You have escaped their hungry clasps. They have failed to bring you down," Dibuseng throws in her own interpretation a split second after I decide to share the reason I suddenly find a watermelon less appetising. "Maybe it was the one we had earlier that left a rather blunt taste in my mouth", I say, trying to forget about the dream.

"I agree with Dibuseng on this one, Maki; this one needs no expert dream interpreter. It's a self-explanatory dream. Your enemies have been defeated. Your prayers have finally been answered. The venomous snakes that were coming for you a while ago, interfering with your peace, are now licking their wounds, with no power to attack you ever again," Modiegi adds with excitement, visibly relieved.

Relieved, I reach for a slice of watermelon and enjoy its sweet juice as I tell the ladies about the tendency of Ms Masego's phone to delete my messages. There's just no taking the madam out of my mind.

We carry on until we're interrupted by a familiar drunken voice echoing behind the irritating sound of feet being dragged. It's Khehla, the mentally challenged guy from the neighbourhood who never seems to miss any of our visits. He walks straight to me and, as expected, attempts to greet me with a kiss. I make a run for it.

His next move is also not so unpredictable.

"Come on, my baby, buy me some cold drink," he says, adding some lyrical praises about how educated we all are and how we can afford to buy him all the drinks he would need for the entire year.

I try to take his attention away from me by offering him a slice of watermelon, which he gently turns down by saying that he would rather take frequent trips to the loo as a result of his beer than being bullied around by a mere watermelon. Khehla would never last a day in my office, and I admire him for his outspokenness. The freedom of the village knows no limits. It is far-reaching and did not discriminate.

20

A yearning for something ... else

I catch the reflection of an unfamiliar older female in the mirror, and after a few moments, I recognise the face staring back as my own. When did I start ageing?

It was as though I had just caught a glimpse of my own mother or my childhood friend's mother. How and when did I even get here? I don't know when ageing happens in a person, but it sure is very sneaky. It lurks in the shadows of life's highways and charges when one is busy with life, thinking not much of it other than the fact that it has been financially catered for when it eventually arrives.

I wonder whether my staying on at my stressful work had accelerated my ageing process. I struggle with the possibility that I would still have failed to recognise my face even if I had stayed with my previous employer.

Even the rest of my body had changed dramatically over what appears to be just one night. My bum and tummy have assumed lives completely of their own.

Had I known how quickly these changes come up, I would have cherished more the shape of my youth. I wouldn't have measured the length and visibility of every stretch mark and the depth of every cellulite bump.

I cannot believe this is me, in my forties, and still slaving about. As an adult, it feels humiliating to have to report to people – rushing through the traffic and being served a few middle fingers in a quest to get to work early to simply appease the unappeasable. One would think there was bread in the oven about to be burnt, as it waited for some of us to rescue it. Should I drop off my kids at school before everyone else is there just to be early for work?

Should I swerve through all the traffic and refuse to make way for the ambulances and emergency cars as they rush to the accident scene that is the very cause of the traffic jam? Or still, should I act like some crazy motorists who follow these cars in the emergency lane under the pretence of them being part of the emergency team? Why do they refuse to notice that I work most of my time at the office and never miss a deadline? This is a hijack of my freedom as an adult. Maybe I should stop demanding this freedom and just take it. But to do that I would have to be independent.

There is nothing as painful as a lack of freedom for an adult. One day, I will look down from heaven at my life on earth, and I will kick myself when I realise with regret that I did not have to waste my life the way I did. That I was made to be free – to work when it was most rewarding and productive for me and those that I serve, and to rest when my body so demanded.

I'm glad though that I was raised by women who had no issues with ageing. For this reason, I often wish I could trade places with the likes of Ms Masego who, at sixty-something, was busy fighting her age, not only by continuing to work in a job she apparently hates despite often boasting that she doesn't need to, but also by reducing the hems of her dresses and skirts by what seems to be a centimetre for every month that passes by.

The older she gets, the shorter her skirts become, the earlier she arrives at work, the later she knocks off, and the nastier she becomes. Had she been this committed during her prime years, we wouldn't be sitting here being criticised for not having done enough for the organisation. I would be the first to accept that a woman has to do what works for her head. But as far as she's concerned, I'm worried. The whole thing of fighting her age is really not funny. Instead of closing shop, packing up and going, she whines about how people are so unfair and even threatens to leave the organisation – not for fulltime sundowners at the beach, but for yet another organisation. I'm worried Ms Masego will not cope well with retirement when it finally kicks what is left of her butt.

Faith had told me about her former manager who, like a dead man refusing to remain dead, often called to reprimand them about work-related issues during his retirement.

The first time she told me this story I almost fell off my chair. Mr Kay's former team were on a work trip to the North West Province when he called one of them ranting about how the team never bothered to inform him when going on trips. "You fail in the simplest gesture of calling and just informing me that you're attending a conference this week. You are seriously naughty, you all. I mean, what would it take for someone to simply pick up the phone and let me know?"

Faith was certain Mr Kay was showing signs of dementia. Apparently, when the former boss saw her and a colleague at the mall during one working day, he did not just bossily raise up his arm to check the time, he went ahead and asked them what in the hell they were doing at the mall during working hours.

Ms Masego, if not careful, might one day find her retired self in a similar position because she seems to define herself around her work. She is her work; she is her position. What is going to happen to her when the system kicks her out soon? She will lose it just thinking about who would take the position she currently holds. I mean, she knows she has absolutely no control there, but still she would make it known just how mammoth her unattractive shoes were for anyone of us to attempt to fill.

Just the other day she was telling us she would be leaving for another organisation because she was so fed up with the Commission. Today she shows us some advertised posts in the newspaper and brags about how seven people have advised her to apply because she was such a suitable candidate it hurt. She carried that around as though it was some stamp of approval, as though anyone even needed validation to apply for posts.

But for this one, I think I can blame her boss because she likes to emphasise that one must never apply for posts at certain levels unless one has been invited to do so. This must have penetrated Ms Masego's permeable skin because she now believes in such craziness, by the look of things.

Where some have backbones of steel, Ms Masego had a paper-thin one, if there was even one to speak of in the first place. Poor thing.

I find myself doodling at home after work. I get worried. My doodling has so far only been reserved to the 'bored-room.' Has work stress infiltrated my life so much that I've begun taking those feelings home?

"What did you draw here, Mom?" Mmarena asks upon noticing my doodling.

I look closely at the picture hoping it would resemble something I can recognise so I could tell my daughter it was just a bad representation of something. But it resembles nothing from the world I know and live in. "It's nothing, my girl," I respond without expecting to be challenged. But I am.

"Mama, everything you draw is something; it cannot be nothing," she surprises me into silence. I'm taken aback by her wisdom, and I nod in agreement. She was right, "*nothing* can never be drawn." I laugh as I imagine her one day challenging me into drawing her, *nothing*.

"The grade sevens are going to prison tomorrow," she continues.

"That's great."

"It is?" she responds with alarm.

"Yes, it is. It will make them aware of where the life of crime leads to. I hope they repeat it year after year. I would be happy if you went on that trip too," I say as I put aside the artwork to focus on some real work that I brought home.

I cannot help to feel discouraged. Last week I got so busy completing a questionnaire that Lalang had sent to me and a few other colleagues from outside the unit, I even stayed late working on it.

But today at the meeting I accidentally learnt by piecing together some information – that as I was promptly working on the questionnaire, Lalang, Leonard, and Maphefo had a brainstorming session of their own on the same document.

Why was I only given this document to complete with external people while they got to discuss and share ideas as a team? If I didn't accept it before that I wasn't regarded as a member of the team, I had to now.

What made me even angrier and sadder was the fact that as I worked on this document well into the wee hours of the morning, the same document had already been discussed and finalised between the three of them.

I only realise as I lie in bed later what Mmarena's alarm and silence at my last statement signalled. In my mind she's is in Grade 6, that's why I told her I would love for her to go on a similar trip when she gets to Grade 7. The problem is, my daughter is in Grade 7, too.

I realise just how foggy my mind had been. I don't think I'll ever recover from the effects of 'pregnancy brain'. Just the day before I caught myself wearing a top on my bra-less body. Precisely the reason there is something called retirement. It seems to be coming down too quickly for me. *I cannot let this job get to me like this, I need some time off to rest and clear my mind, I think, before dozing off.*

21

Weighing up pains

The orange was so dry I could have set it on fire, and it would have completely caught and burnt down to ashes. But I sucked on that thing as though there was plenty of juice in it.

Oranges, chilled mangoes and boiled eggs have literally kept me alive for the past week post-surgery. I resent my bathroom scale for having only moved down a lousy one hundred grams since the surgery. All this semi-eating is not nearly doing as much harm as I would have preferred it to. I have been cheated. This was supposed to be the easiest and quickest route to looking like a supermodel. I had gotten a raw deal for all my pain.

I begin to question whether food was really the reason for my full figure and whether the old ladies back at my home village might have been right when they insisted that fat had very little to do with food but everything to do with the heart – with contentment.

My grandmother's reverence for cellulite had gone a long way in helping me establish a healthy relationship with my body and accept myself as I was. But the flip side was very real. I wonder how utterances such as "fat is royalty" and that she had wanted to be meaty her entire life but it eluded her, had worked at our subconscious to stay as far as possible from the gym. "Whenever a chubby person is without clothing, it is pleasing on the eye, and when a skinny woman gets old, people will refer to her as that skinny little old lady, but when a chubby one is old, she will only be referred to as the old lady". Granted, affirmations like these helped one to accept one's seemingly natural stoutness. But would I ever know how her words conspired to push me to be overweight?

Maybe gran knew exactly what she was doing. It's not like she never teased us about the same fat. Perhaps that was her true stance on the matter. She probably encouraged some meat, but not huge stacks of it.

But there are things I've already gained as a result of the tonsillectomy — things such as being far away from the office and from Ms Masego. Not to mention being rid of the annoying tonsilliths. I've had tonsiliths, or tonsil stones, for as long as I can remember brushing my teeth.

As a young girl, I was fascinated by these small white stinky stuff that came out of my mouth at times when I brushed my teeth. There seemed to be some sort of unspoken rule of dealing with these smelly whitish things: when you smell one from the back of your mouth, try whatever you can to get it out, and if it falls you've got to pick it up. Then crush it between your fingers while anticipating the foul odour. Take your finger to your nose and sniff in the undeniably smelly thing, because even though you've been smelling them forever, you just can never let one go without smelling it.

It must have been the disbelief that something so small could have such a strong, unique and somewhat compelling odour that kept me doing this over and over and over again. I don't think there's any other unpleasant smelling matter that's as sneaky and irresistible to sniff. I cannot believe that I miss them already. I even shed a tear as I come to terms with the reality of living without them.

It's something of a shock that I could miss something that made me so self-conscious whenever I could smell it in my throat but was unable to take it out. Then a thought crosses my mind. Would I ever miss Ms Masego if she decided to heed the call of retirement and left? I assure myself that it wasn't possible for me to ever miss her. But who knows? Bad and sometimes evil as she may be, she never stuck to my throat and was certainly not as bad smelling.

I also think of my tonsils. I meant it when I asked the nurse before surgery whether I could say goodbye to them. But she just laughed and told me that it was against the Tissues Act or something and that all tissues needed to be discarded immediately and in a particular manner. But my request must have touched her because she used that unusual request of mine to wake me up from the anaesthetic. "Oh, there she is; she wanted to say goodbye to her tonsils." I smiled. She confirmed that I remembered my request correctly and that I didn't lose any screws during the procedure. I was fine.

The excruciating pain I feel in my throat and in my ears force my winding mind back to my reality. It didn't matter what I lost and what I didn't lose or what closure I wasn't afforded, I was dealing with pain that makes labour pains seem like a round of Pilates. All this pain for Ms Masego! For taking a break from her! No, it was actually bigger and more effective than that at the end. I should be glad that the operation went well despite my doctor scaring me about the anaesthesia, instead of alleviating my fears. When I shared about my fear of the operating theatre and that I might not wake up, my good doctor responded in a manner I couldn't have anticipated. I had asked with the hope that the good old doctor would reassure me of the safety of the procedure, but I was wrong. He was not about to be conventional just to make me feel better.

"You're right; theatres are very scary places. You can only hope that the guy who puts you out is okay enough up there and that he will be able to bring you back," he said casually, oblivious to my wide-open, half-dumbfounded and half-amused mouth. And as though he'd just realised what he just let on, he wrapped up with "but we make sure to use anaesthetists who are in a good frame of mind."

His last statement made me feel a little better ... it had to make me feel better because there was simply no turning back on my decision to have the operation done.

My research into the possible consequences of holding on to rotten tonsils informed me that I could wake up one day with a haemorrhage that could be very dangerous.

And with me being such a worrywart, if it could happen to anyone, it would happen to me. That was one side of the motivation.

If I died on that operating table, Ms Masego would never know how the thought of evading her had given me the courage to have the procedure done. Draining people like Ms Masego can drive one into opting for surgeries that one had put on hold for ages, just so one can get a few days off work. She was more motivation than the tonsil stones and being told by the doctor how rotten my tonsils were.

The allure of getting two weeks off Ms Masego became too sweet to resist. So after making the doctor swear on his mother's grave that this surgery requires at least two weeks to heal, I had finally scheduled an appointment for the dreaded surgery.

But the pain I'm now feeling makes me wonder if the procedure was worth it. Would I rather endure physical pain like this forever than work with Ms Masego? *Maybe she wasn't such a pain in the ear, after all*, I think as I drive so slow to my post-surgery appointment that I had to question whether my mouth was supposed to be somehow involved in the act of driving. I ignore the impatient drivers as they hoot. I am glad that I am a patient person on the road because I know that what a fellow driver might be going through for them to be "slow or idiotic" drivers, I do not know.

It gives little comfort that the doctor says my wound is healing beautifully. I'm still in pain and have consumed more painkillers in the past week than I had my entire life. At the end, I only get to enjoy the last few days of my sick leave when I finally get delivered from the pain.

I should have fallen pregnant to get at least four months off Lalang, I think as I enter the office building after a very short two weeks off. Just being a few metres away from her makes me think of trying for another baby to get a four-month break. The shameful reasons we bring innocent souls into this universe!

* * *

I must have attracted the surprise pregnancy. If not by secretly wishing for it to happen so I could take a break from Lalang for a couple of months, then by trying to go back to complete my master's degree. The degree is already spanning more than a decade and two babies. My promoter at varsity laughed when I said to him, as I discovered that I was pregnant yet again during my second return to varsity to complete my thesis, that Master degrees cause pregnancy.

"If I was in doubt about this fact before, I'm not any more. Maybe my babies are my true Master degrees – my two-eyed masters. I sure know a lot of mothers would agree," I had said.

I meet up with the professor on my way to my first consultation with the gynaecologist since discovering the pregnancy three weeks ago. "Well, I suppose all good things come in threes," he says. I agree. That must have been reason number three why this pregnancy was bound to happen. I admire families with three kids, especially when they're all the same gender. I don't know where this admiration comes from, but it always gave me a wish dilemma – wishing for a third on the one hand and being okay with two on the other. We agree that pregnancy shouldn't deter me this time around because all the coursework was already done. With just the thesis remaining, I will do as much as I can during the next couple of months. Hopefully, this pregnancy treats me just as well as the first two. I feel better about my prospects as I bid goodbye to my promoter and head to my appointment with the gynaecologist.

But what is wrong with these doctors to tell it like it is? Was pain and death so natural to them that they have lost any sense of how the rest of us feel about such things? First it was the ear, nose and throat doctor confirming to me how risky the tonsillectomy was; now it is the obstetrician reminding me of something I do not need to be reminded of: how I hated the invasive foetal examinations and how I had quickly pushed baby number two out before the doctor made his way to the ward.

He insists that I pushed quickly to avoid him and his big hand checking me after the nurse's softer one had already. I had to admit that after experiencing the nurse's softer hand in that delivery room, I knew for the first time that it had been his massive hand that made the procedure unbearable.

"You have just reminded me of a vow I took since that discovery about hand sizes," I blurt out.

"What was it?" The doctor asks almost with some apprehension.

"I promised myself that should I put myself through this gruesome process called childbirth ever again, I was going to change to a softer-handed obstetrician. But here I am again, facing the same big hand I had run from the last time. Just as I had forgotten how painful labour was and gotten myself pregnant again, I had also forgotten just how important hand size is in this whole process."

"You got yourself pregnant!" he laughs. "I have to say your husband is quite busy wasting you away; you were a young, first time preggie when I first met you."

"But seriously now, Doctor, are you telling me that medical science with all its technological advances hasn't come up with a better alternative to this hand invasion thingy?"

"I kid you not, Mrs Mako. The only alternative would be if I put my head in there to check with my eyes," he says with a serious face as I burst out laughing at this totally unpalatable idea.

Even as I laugh, his message could not have been louder: there are no alternatives to the pelvic examinations by hand. I know now that the only thing to do is to put on my big girl panties, grin and bear the nasty handwork. I manage to smile as my thoughts drift to the office ... and Lalang's face flashes in sight.

"You know what, Doctor, you can do as many pelvic examinations as you want. Even those are better than being in that woman's company."

"Who's the unlucky person you loathe that much?"

"I really don't loathe anyone; it's she who's demonstrated a loathing for me. Suffice to say it's someone who sure is going to make the labour feel like a walk in the park. I will push harder thinking of her than I ever would thinking of that big hand of yours."

22

Baby blues

The alarm clock rudely wakes me with a distressing sound like that of an ambulance siren.

Makhananisa is already in the shower. Thanks to his internal alarm clock he never needs to wake up to such horrific sounds. I usually set the alarm ten minutes after my desired wake-up time, as a back-up in case I do not wake up by myself. But I always get to the 'just in case' time. I stopped my husband from waking me up because he does so too early. I hate parting with my blankets, and over the years this has kept me fixated on that day in the future when I wouldn't have to wake up to an alarm.

As I jump out of bed to switch the alarm off, Baby wakes up. What was I thinking setting an alarm!? I should revert to asking my hubby to wake me up so I could take a quick bath before Baby wakes up and demands his feed.

Now I have to just calm down, forget about rigid working times and calmly feed him so that he falls asleep again. The nanny will arrive any minute now, and I will be able to hand the baby over to her if he doesn't fall asleep first.

My anxiety is difficult to control; I can feel my heart breaking into pieces as my baby sucks too close to it. No matter how hard I try, I cannot get it to beat slower. At this rate, there is no way Baby is going to fall asleep as quickly as I want him to.

I'm growing increasingly anxious and irritated with the nine-to-five life. I work with an older woman who seems to have conveniently forgotten what it's like to have to wear breast pads and feel your breasts fill up in the middle of a presentation.

Then you worry about whether your baby might be crying back home, while you pray that your breast pads will hold enough liquid so that it doesn't pass through and start showing on your white blouse! And while I can somewhat get used to Lalang's inflexible approach as far as working hours are concerned, and her selective rule-bound behaviour, I still find it hard to believe that she actually never asked me about the baby.

What mother, especially what grandmother would be so cold toward one person they cannot even warm up to a baby? If I can be civil enough to say 'happy birthday' to her, surely she could still find it in her heart somewhere to have said 'congratulations' when I texted her about the baby, or even to simply ask 'how's the baby?' when I returned to work.

After forever had come and gone, Baby finally falls asleep. My helpless baby has to suck on such heaviness. I lay him down as quietly as I can, my irritation growing at my husband who was doing his usual whistling as he prepared himself. At this point I'm unsure whether it's more his whistling or the fact that I can't shout at him to stop, that's getting to my nerves.

"Is he asleep? I was thinking I'll watch him so you can bath, but I guess I should get going now or I'll be late for my meeting," he says, prompting me to snap at him about how he could not nurse the baby even if he watched him and how I can't bear to hear him cry while I take a bath, knowing full well I'm going to be away from him for a full day, every work day.

"But, Honey, I suggested that we introduce him to the bottle so that you also get some relief, and you refused. Is it now my fault that God decided it would not be the man who grows boobs to breastfeed his babies?"

"Just go. You cannot even take me to work on a day like this, and you expect me to drive myself while I'm stressed out as I am!"

"Again, I suggested to you that you ask for additional leave for the week so that I could start to take you to work from next week. It's just not possible for me to do it this week. I don't know why you have to be so hard headed about going back to work. I'm sure your manager would have understood; you've just returned from maternity leave, for crying out loud."

"I'm sorry. It's okay, Mariam will be here any minute now should the baby wake up as I get ready."

By the Grace of God, I finish my bath without him waking up. I just have to pray that he doesn't wake up before I get dressed. I manage to put one leg into my pants. I look up to give thanks for that achievement as I put the other leg in. "Thank you, Lord." Baby sleeping through while I take a bath is always worthy of a celebration. I know all about being whisked from my bath with soaking wet feet to pay attention to screaming little ones.

I wish I was a citizen in one of those countries that give women a full twelve months of maternity leave. Or at least six months. I cannot believe how quickly the four months went by. I was only starting to recover from the baby blues and the slight post-natal depression and was starting to enjoy my baby.

Now I have to go to work and leave my little baby in the hands of someone who is practically a stranger. I've heard and read about so many horror stories relating to nannies – so many that even my faith fails me.

I have to start looking for daycare centres despite my friends and family members' discouragement and criticism of this choice. I've done it before, and it worked for me.

"With a school, if they abuse them they will be abused as a group. Unlike in the house alone with an abusive minder," I keep repeating my grandmother's view as I try and convince myself that daycare is the best option for my precious baby.

I shed a tear over the fact that at baby number three, I still find myself unprepared to be a full-time mom. Makhananisa insists that we are ready, but my assessment tells me we will only be ready in another three years or so. I would hate to make a miscalculation of our financial situation. Life carries too many stressors; I believe finances does not have to be one of them.

I jump into my car, which in my husband's words, "resembles a construction vehicle with all the plans and even soil samples aboard". But mine resembles a mother's, I would insist. With all the scattered socks, breast pads, wet wipes, vests – some of which I have to move from the driver' seat before I can even manage to get inside.

Though I'm stressed out about my second day at work, I'm nonetheless happy with my life. I giggle as I recall my boy, Motheo's words: "I thank God for my life, my family and everything. I may be missing a few of my teeth, but that doesn't mean I cannot be happy". His words have become something of a mantra to me.

If you're a human being on this earth, you will, whether you like it or not, unintentionally tread on ants. What good would it do if all the ants you stepped on were to get angry and hated you unto death for something you don't even know you've done?

It's not Lalang's fault that I have a baby; it's a blessing. My blessing. It's not my husband's fault that I have not gotten off my backside and started to make my long-time dream of building a nursery school a reality. Three babies and I'm still not set up. I had wished with each pregnancy that I would not have to return to work, but I had not done the necessary groundwork. I guess it will be my grandchildren who'll get to attend my state-of-the-art crèche one day.

23

Work Blues

Trust madam Lalang to put undue pressure on us. She only suggested four days ago that we read this strategic management book and now she's putting pressure on us by telling us how she read the entire book in just two days and that she woke up at 3am to finish it.

Of course she doesn't spare a thought for those of us who did not sleep a wink because the baby was feverish. How could she know that shortly after getting home at six yesterday evening, I had to take the baby to the emergency room at the hospital and that we only got home after eight?

And how could she ever know that one young mother would never wake up at such crazy hours because her baby doesn't ever fall asleep before 2am? She must have had very good babies over twenty years ago that her sleeping clock was never once interrupted, or like many women managers with older kids, she had conveniently forgotten all about it.

As I feel everyone's eyes fixated on me, I hear Madam's voice call my name. She must have been calling for a while because her voice sounded raised, and why would everyone be looking at me like that if she only called me for the first time? As I park my dreamy thoughts and my slumbering and turn to listen, she asks if I've read the book.

"I read the first chapter on the first evening," I respond calmly, succeeding to conceal the sadness I was feeling that here I am, a mother with a four month old colicky baby at home, being asked if I'd finished a 'prescribed' book in less than a week!

I really cannot do this working thing; it's the ultimate freedom stealer. How could I, a grown adult, have my life controlled like this by people who don't give a damn about my circumstances?" I think to myself as Lalang continues to zap away not just my freedom but my very life too.

"You'll have time tonight to finish it because you'll be away from home. Tomorrow morning we must be in Cape Town for a meeting – you and me," she continues. "It's an urgent one, and the executive want us to be there because it's related to that research you conducted before you went on maternity leave."

"Oh, just please shoot me right now!" I think to myself as I get more and more annoyed at how I was not in control of my life. My life wasn't mine – not as long as I was employed. I'm lost for words.

Just when I think my burdens couldn't get worse, another mission is piled on. How could I be expected to leave my nursing baby for a night? Would my husband cope? How is he going to feel when I call him and tell him I'm packing and leaving, and that I won't be there when he gets home in the evening?

Where do I begin telling him that? I don't know what else was said or discussed during the rest of the meeting as I had gone out of my body to go throw myself a massive pity party.

When I started working, I observed other mothers suffer similar predicaments, and I had sworn to myself that by the time my husband and I start a family, my financial and business affairs would be in order so I wouldn't have to return to work after maternity leave. The tiredness, the longing for their babies back home, the anxiety about whether they were receiving proper care from their caregivers, the porridge brain caused by pregnancy and exacerbated by sleep deprivation and exhaustion, all opened my eyes to the realities of working mothers, especially those that were new to motherhood.

For at least five years I saved like a squirrel, hoping that this would one day afford me the luxury of being a stay-at-home mother. I invested wisely, hoping this would be sufficient to supplement a single salary as I worked on my life-long dream of owning a crèche. For this dream, we both lived frugally. It was fear that pushed me back to work after my first maternity leave was over. After all, many other mothers continued to work out of the home, despite the challenges.

I shouldn't have returned to work after this maternity leave. I planned so meticulously for the first two that it doesn't make sense at all that more than a decade later I find myself not ready to be my own boss and raise my third baby full-time. How could things have turned out so differently? If only I wasn't so risk-averse! I can make more money working for myself as I have so many good income generating ideas.

I'm a bit envious of my two former colleagues who've taken the leap of faith and left the rat race. When I finally leave, I'll be more like Manare who works from home with multiple streams of income. Tilly, on the other hand, literally sits at home after having decided to leave her toxic job. With a full-time helper, all Tilly has to worry about is what colour she's going to paint her nails on her next visit to the beauty salon and which among her lingerie would put a beautiful end to her already perfect day. *If I were* in Tilly's position, I would probably build a small empire. I continue to daydream.

When I return from my 'meeting with myself', I realise I had missed the rest of Madam's brief about this unexpected trip.

I know I'll be overlooked for the next promotion and for any performance incentive anyway, so I say what I need to say: "Madam, I don't know how to say this to make you understand my dilemma, but I'm actually a breastfeeding mother to a four-month-old baby at the moment; I don't have a full-time nanny, and if at all possible I would like to be excused from this trip."

My words are followed by moments of silence, making me wonder if I truly did utter the words, or perhaps in my sleep-deprived state I thought I was talking while in fact, I was just thinking. Faith's words confirm that I did actually say something.

"Madam Masego, if it's okay with you, I will go on Maki's behalf. I've worked with her on this project, and I can do the presentation. I know that not only is Maki breastfeeding, but her baby hasn't been well lately. I know how hard it can be when one has a baby. Her husband has also been unwell."

I could have stood up right there and kissed this angelic girl who has become more of a sister than a colleague. It sounded so much better coming from her than it would have coming entirely from me. Madam would probably have been a lot colder if there weren't so many people in the room. She agrees to Faith's suggestion but asks that we have a chat after the meeting.

I thank Faith after the meeting, and we laugh about the extra sauce she added about my husband being unwell. "You know she values husbands more than babies," Faith says.

I follow Lalang to her office where I receive a full lecture about being serious as a career woman.

"We all had to leave our babies with nannies. You cannot have your cake and eat it. Either you're a working mother, or you're a stay-at-home mother; but you cannot be both," Lalang says.

I cannot be bothered about the lecture. I just want to get out of the meeting and beat the rush hour traffic back to my baby.

Personally, I think Lalang is just trying to make my life difficult because she has previously let even the likes of Maphefo present at similar platforms, on this very project, which Faith and myself worked our heads off on. She has allowed them to use our presentation in secret and to go present outside of the organisation.

I get home, put baby to breast and watch a show about people who escaped prison, as baby falls asleep right away. I notice just how we all have a deep yearning for freedom as human beings. I even catch myself biting my nails as police close down on an escapee.

This scares me. How could I be connecting with a criminal who belongs in jail, and actually hold my breath hoping he succeeds in his escape? I forgive myself as I realise that I've forgiven the prisoner; I have forgiven him because he showed remorse and seemed like a completely new person.

I imagine that it's reasonable that every imprisoned person would constantly be thinking of ways to attain their freedom. I relate because I too am in prison; I'm in prison because my freedom belongs to someone else. The person trying to escape is doing what all of us strive for – going after his freedom. I don't condone his criminal ways, I just can relate to the feeling of being told what to do, when and how to do it.

Our freedom is ours to strive for. I let go of any resentment of Makhananisa not pushing me enough to get out of the rat race trap because I realise at that moment that this was not his baby to nurse.

The one that bears the wound is the one that must nurse and scratch it, for only they would know where and when it itches and how much pressure to apply when scratching.

Asking someone else to scratch when you can scratch yourself could at best cause dissatisfaction and at worst, serious harm. He has supported my idea of quitting; it was unfair to expect him to apply pressure too.

I carry Baby a while longer as he let go of the nipple. I watch him smile in his sleep. He seems much better than he was earlier. I'm grateful that I'm here with him this evening and not out of town in some indifferent hotel room. I pray that there won't be any need for me to travel anytime soon.

24

Coping mechanisms

"Mama, are babies born out of the tummy or out of the private part?" Motheo asks just before I drop them off at school. *Oh my, are these the type of conversations Makhananisa has to deal with during the commute these days?* I wonder. I haven't done the school run since the last trimester in my pregnancy.

Before I could manage to close my wide-open mouth and bring my lips together so I could mumble some sort of response, he continues: "I always thought they came out of the tummy, but in the movies, they show them coming out of the private part. I cannot imagine how that could even be possible. Babies are so big. Does the private part get bigger for the birth and then get back to its normal size afterwards?"

I manage to contain myself. "It is all kinda natural, my boy. Does it not surprise you that the tummy gets bigger to accommodate the size of the baby as it grows? Anyway, some questions should be answered through experience. You will understand when it's the right time."

"And what about us, were we taken out of the tummy or the private part?" he continues.

I laugh so hard ... more because of being dumbfounded than finding this whole thing comical. His usually talkative sister is dead silent. Obviously somewhat embarrassed.

"You are natural babies. You should know Mama likes all things natural."

A sudden sadness engulfs me as I forge a smile and kiss them goodbye. I'm sad because my spirit badly yearns for my days to be exactly like this. I want to be able to engage in mindless and stimulating conversations while driving the kids to school, without having to worry about the time and what mood Ms Masego would be in and how the rest of my day will go.

I want to drop the kids off and go home to take care of my baby and do whatever other business my heart and head would have me do for that day.

I sigh as I wake up to the fact that I'm not driving back home, but am yet again headed to that same place I would rather not be in. I'm headed to that same company of certain unpleasant people I would rather not be spending my precious time with. Where on earth is my freedom in all of this? I know there is none.

I've told Makhananisa many times that I feel not like an adult with choices, but a child who has absolutely no control over some of her life decisions.

I turn right at a moment's decision, instead of left. I am going back home first. I just want to feel, just this once, like I was not going to work. I will call in late today; there's no bread waiting to be baked by me, and there is certainly no one that could possibly die because I happen to be craving life today.

I will do as I please today and I will do it slowly, like a stay-at-home mother in no hurry to get anywhere. I treat myself to some nice music, and I escape.

I get home to find baby still sleeping. I make myself a nice cup of hot chocolate, sit out on the patio and wonder why on earth the patio is so underutilised. Who was it build for when we spend all this time away from home? No wonder one feels so out of balance. Nice things like this are meant to be enjoyed more frequently.

I notice how Mariam looks at me from the corners of her eyes, obviously wondering what in the world I was doing at my house this time of the morning because I didn't tell her of any leave for today.

I'm sorry for being here and disturbing your peace, Mariam dearest. Dare I remind you whose house this is! You're the one enjoying it every single day, and I cannot get to enjoy it just this once without feeling as though I was encroaching on your territory? Look, I already know that you treat yourself to a scrumptious bacon and egg breakfast every morning while I gobble my quick and convenient peanut butter sandwich. Why won't you go ahead and ignore me? Pretend I'm not here and fix yourself a nice breakfast instead of making me so uncomfortable to be enjoying my own space this once.

I'm not used to having someone in the house sharing my personal space. But juggling work, wifely and motherly duties only took me up to a point and almost drove me to the edge. With baby number three, something had to give.

It took me a long time of comprehending what it would be like having someone in the house during the day. I had managed to raise the older ones without a nanny, and it was getting easier each passing day as they grew to be less demanding. But I had to get a helper at the end because with Baby around, and no trusted crèche close by anymore, I had little choice.

I sit and fantasise a bit about that day Faith and I commonly fantasise about. The day Lalang finally retires. *Can't I for once just take Lalang out of my mind!* I reprimand myself before going right ahead.

Faith and I would gracefully miss her farewell party and go celebrate somewhere on our own. Ours would not be about the freedom to do as we please, but we will celebrate the birth of our true potential that would have some chance of being applied without people shooting at our ideas and our beings. It would be a celebration of being true thought leaders. It would be the end of travelling for the sake of spending money lest someone is seen as inefficient. It would be a chance to spend money doing meaningful work that would hopefully make a difference; an end of working for the sake of keeping busy. We dream of that day when we would raise our glasses to a new dawn and an end to intentionally burying and hiding errors deep inside reports and laying sugary icing on them because "they hardly ever read past the first few pages".

That would be a beautiful day. But while that day would free up some of the unnecessary data in my head and make me more productive, it doesn't seem to be something that will happen soon.

But more than anything, I long for the day when I will be able to sit out in this same spot and sip elegantly on my mood's choice of beverage - as slowly as my lips would permit. I look forward to a time when I will be able to play with Baby, or sit and fantasise about what to prepare for dinner.

I would regularly visit my favourite spa for a well-deserved treat, or retreat somewhere to watch praying mantes mate, not having a care about where under the charmingly hot African sun could the likes of Lalang Masego possibly be, nor recalling I have ever known her.

And until the time comes when I'm truly free, I will just keep on happily collecting all the lemons thrown my way, and instead of swallowing them like bitter medicine while wrinkling my face in the process from all the frowning, I will take them and continue to make lemonade.

— The End —